Last

Lily Greene

Copyright © Lily Greene 2015

The right of Lily Greene to be identified as the author of this work has been asserted by her in accordance with the Copyright, Designs and Patents Act, 1988.

First published in 2015 by Endeavour Press Ltd.

Table of Contents

Chapter One

Chapter Two

Chapter Three

Chapter Four

Chapter Five

Chapter Six

Chapter Seven

Chapter Eight

Chapter Nine

Chapter Ten

Chapter Eleven

Chapter Twelve

Chapter One

As Ella slipped past an old man, crawling forward at a tortoise-like pace, she eyed up the last basket that had longed to feel the embrace of a frenzied Christmas shopper. She picked up the basket stacked patiently next to the trolleys, slung it over her arm and marched through the parting doors in one graceful swoop. The force of the heating inside the door made her coat billow around her and she revelled in the new warmth.

Ella Moore always looked glamorous. Her cheek bones were set high upon her face and her lips were rosy and plump. She had the air of a movie star about her as she sauntered through the supermarket in a sleek midnight blue coat. Her body was voluptuous, in a way that wasn't in fashion anymore, and she knew how to use her curves to devastating effect. Ella was an artist, and despite the odd flick of paint on her sophisticated clothes, she always looked chic. She had no interest in high fashion brands but she had style.

Now in the shelter of the supermarket, Ella tried to dry her curly hair with her hands. It had been raining in London since breakfast and Ella had forgotten her umbrella and been caught unprepared. Her rich brown locks spilled over the white fur headband she wore to keep her ears warm. Normally Ella straightened her curls but if there was a slight chance of rain there was no point. She blew a strand of hair away from her chestnut coloured eyes and focused on her shopping.

Ella rubbed her frozen cheeks, as she steamed past the groceries and into the second aisle. She was on a mission. Her best friend Libby and her family, the Crosleys, were hosting a party that evening in the countryside. She only had a few hours to shop, get ready and drive out to the depths of Kent before the party started and she had been given strict instructions from Libby not to be late. If there was one thing Ella knew, nay feared, about her best friend, it was not to disregard Libby's military-like precision and regard for punctuality.

Ella pulled out a list from her coat pocket detailing the items she needed to buy; Christmas cards, hairspray, champagne, and icing sugar to finish off the mince pies she had prepared for the party. She found the stationery section first and decided to tease Libby by picking out a card that she knew she would hate. Libby would be stressed about the party and Ella thought that a dose of humour would do her the world of good. They had always teased each other like this in a sisterly way and it helped that Ella knew Libby's specific dislikes. She selected a card which showed dreary looking angels with large pancake-shaped heads peering out from behind a tinsel-studded tree. Libby hated tinsel. *Perfect*. A smirk spread across Ella's face as she imagined the distasteful look and then laughter that would follow the opening of the garish card. She picked up another more traditional and classier card; a water-colour of families ice-skating around a big frozen pond. The children dressed in Victorian smocks and scarves looked serene in the snow and Ella thought it would do nicely for Elisabeth and William, Libby's parents.

Ella turned the corner of the aisle to find her next item when she was struck by a luminescent display of Christmas lights and decorations all propped up on a tier of tables. The sight was magical; there were wreaths of intricately intertwined fairy lights, twigs of mistletoe, handmade Christmas crackers covered in glitter, and angel figurines with long flowing locks and glowing halos. In the middle of the display, some small stuffed Father Christmas dolls sat cheerily. The portly Santas were surrounded by straw and lodged in what looked like a crib. They looked bizarre next to the elegant wreaths, especially as they were taking up the place usually reserved for baby Jesus, but the overall look was sweetly festive and brought a smile to Ella's now slightly less frozen face.

Ella owed her love of Christmas to her parents who had been mad about the holiday. Swinging the basket on her arm and staring at the display, she remembered fondly that her father used to play Christmas songs all year round. It was normal to catch him singing 'Deck the Halls' while mowing the lawn in April and her mother would often start making Christmas crackers as early as August. This was one of the many things that Ella missed about her parents. They had died tragically in a car crash five years ago and although it pained her to be without them at Christmas, she counted herself lucky to have such treasured memories of them.

Ella managed to tear her eyes away from the spectacular display and headed to the cosmetic aisle to pick up her second item; hairspray. She plopped an industrial sized can of L'Oreal Elnett into her basket and soldiered on through the supermarket.

Walking down the length of the shop where all the aisles met the delicatessen counter, Ella could see a chirpy saleswoman at the far end, giving away free samples. Without her glasses, she couldn't see what it was this rather pretty and very busty blonde woman was offering. As she advanced on the stall, the promotional sign became clearer. "Sleep like a log, after a glass of Eggnog". Ella sniggered at the cheesy marketing.

"Free taste?" asked the doe-eyed sales assistant, whose lip-gloss was almost as shiny as the Christmas lights hanging above her head.

What is eggnog? Isn't it some sort of bizarre concoction of egg and porridge? Probably incredibly sweet, Ella deduced, remembering its American origins. She made a mental note to ask Annie, her friend from Chicago, what eggnog was made of, when suddenly, Robbie's face popped into her head.

He is probably drinking a glass of eggnog right now with his new woman in some fashionable apartment in downtown Chicago ... The thought soured Ella's taste buds. She tried to drive the image from her mind and prevent resentment dampening her Christmas spirit.

"No, thank you," replied Ella. "I'm in a bit of a rush but it looks delicious!"

She forced a smile as she walked away from the tasting stand and tried to think of something other than Robbie. But it was no use. For the first time, she thought about what it would feel like to be single at Christmas this year. To be without Robbie. She had spent the last five Christmases with him and his family. Since her parents had passed away, she and Robbie had created extravagant, fun and silly holiday traditions and this year, without even her brother who was away on business, she would be alone. Bitterly alone.

Ella headed to the dried goods aisle to find icing sugar.

Perhaps instead of shopping for sugar, I should be shopping for a man ... No Ella!

She was determined not to become Bridget Jones; she knew she must avoid wholesale-sized tubs of ice cream and karaoke nights with aging work colleagues. No good could come from attempting to drunkenly sing both parts of a duet. She should also steer clear of beige pants that were big enough to use as a sail. Or perhaps she *should* buy a pair and use them to float down the river Thames on a one-way trip to spinsterhood.

No, Ella was determined not to take on the crazy cat lady identity just yet. She was only twenty-nine years old after all. So what if she was single? She had her health, youth, and talent. She had a good job at the prestigious Triangle Gallery, she was exhibiting her paintings at the trendy new Beat Gallery in a weeks' time – her first ever exhibition! And she had recently bought a flat in North London. She had every reason to be happy.

Ella awoke from her pathetic pep talk to see a tall, broad shouldered man standing a few paces in front of her. He was staring at the coffee and although he had his back to her, she could see from his profile that he had a strong jaw-line, a chiselled roman nose and thick dark blonde hair. He was gorgeous. Ella pretended to be interested in the ingredients of a pot of cocoa powder as the Blonde Haired man turned to face her. When he swivelled around he revealed a bright festive jumper; a gleeful reindeer expanded the width of his torso and it stared at Ella with its two googly eyes, placed inappropriately over his nipples. The unfortunate placing of the eyes was accompanied by a flashing red nose plonked straight where Ella imagined his belly button must be.

Ella could not help but giggle. The man looked ridiculous.

What is this, wearable technology?

She tried to stifle her laugh to stop this man from suffering any further embarrassment and attempted to turn her throaty cackle into a cough. Just as she started to feign a coughing fit, a lithe red-headed woman came out from behind her, linked arms with the now red-in-the-face Blonde Haired man, and stalked off down the aisle, dragging him with her.

Ella felt a little mean for laughing at the poor man's attire, which his wife had made him wear no doubt, but she detested Christmas jumpers. She adored Christmas and all festive decorations, but there was something about a Christmas jumper that made her skin crawl; they were ugly and cheap and were only worn by people desperate to prove how easy-going and funny they were. Ella's pitiful ex-boss, Tim Collins, used to wear them at work Christmas parties; he wore them to show he was a 'fun time guy' who was mates with his employees. But really he was a balding middle-aged man, whose eagerness to laugh at his own jokes and relentless attempts to seduce much younger coworkers made him unbearable to work alongside. He was who Ricky Gervais' fictional character David Brent *must* have been based on. In Ella's eyes, Christmas jumpers were almost certainly the most deplorable aspect of Christmas.

Ella picked up a small packet of icing sugar next to the cocoa she'd been fondling and made her way towards the alcohol aisle. She passed the wines and stopped at the Champagne. Did Libby prefer Moët or Veuve Clicquot? She couldn't remember and she couldn't afford to buy either until more of her paintings sold. But Ella, spurred on by Christmas spirit, placed a bottle of Moët in her basket and decided to use her credit card.

Just as she was thinking about the evening ahead, a mother holding hands with a small waddling child walked past her. The boy was carrying a toy train and was producing enthusiastic sound effects to match the rolling motions he was using it to make. The little boy, who was about five years old, steamed towards Ella when he saw her. Using the train as a prop and crying "Choo chooooo", the boy reached out his arm and ran the toy train around the hem of Ella's coat. Ella smiled at the little boy, whose podgy face looked positively angelic.

"Hello!" Ella said looking down at the boy.

The mother sighed and rushed forward.

"I am so sorry. He's a little obsessed with trains right now as you can see! Danny, remember not to run into people please," the lady said looking at her son.

Ella reassured the mother that the child was adorable.

Ella turned to the young boy and crouched down so that she was the same height as him. "I like your train. It's very beautiful. Are you excited about Christmas?" she asked. The little boy said nothing, but nodded his head, his big watery eyes staring up at her.

"And what would you like for Christmas?"

"Trrrains," he replied.

"See, trains trains trains!" the mother chortled. "Say goodbye to the lovely lady Danny and wish the man a Merry Christmas." *The man?* The chubby cheeked boy mumbled "Godbye and Mewwy Christmas," not taking his eyes off Ella's face. He almost stumbled into a display of Christmas chocolates as he tottered away from Ella, but his mother guided him in the right direction just in time to prevent a calamity.

Ella stood up and waved the train enthusiast goodbye. She smiled down at her basket, checking she had all that she needed, and on realising she had finished her shop she turned back towards the checkouts.

But instead of seeing a spotty uniformed shop assistant sunk in a distant checkout chair, Ella saw a beautiful man whose face was less than half a metre away from hers. There was only his basket between them and it touched her knees, blocking her way. Ella was so shocked at seeing this man so close to her that she let out a small high-pitched squeak. His still and calm stature gave no signs of having recently moved and he had clearly been just behind her throughout her encounter with the mother and child.

A small embarrassed smile spread across the stranger's handsome face and he looked shy. The stranger looked like he was in his late thirties. He had chocolate brown hair and his thick, masculine stubble was silvery in the places it was not auburn.

She felt weak at the slightest hint of his smile and her whole body tingled as she stood facing the Brown Haired stranger. He looked like someone she knew, *but who*?

Ella started to smile but just as the gorgeous Brown Haired man began to speak, a mobile ringing pierced the air. Ella realised that the furious sound was coming from her handbag; she put her basket down and rummaged through her suede bag, hoping to retrieve the phone and stifle its noise. She was irritated that it had distracted her from talking to this gorgeous stranger, but when she retrieved her phone and looked up, the Brown Haired man was gone.

Ella answered her iPhone with a curt "Hello?"

"Darling, hi!" Libby screeched down the phone. "Major disaster, you must help me! I need you!"

"Oh Libby, it's you. How are you? How's everything going with the party?" Ella asked as she scanned the alcohol area, trying to spot the Brown Haired man.

"Awful! Didn't I just say? I'm stressing out because Marcus is coming."

"Marcus is coming? Why on earth is Marcus coming?" Ella asked surprised but distracted.

"Because I'm a bloody idiot and when I bumped into him the other day I panicked and I invited him, that's why."

"Oh gosh. Well, don't panic. You've seen him many times since you broke up. It won't be as bad as you're imagining it to be." Ella walked back through the supermarket but there was no trace of the Brown Haired man.

She gave up her search and wondered to the bakery section. If Marcus was going to be at the party tonight then Libby would need cheering up and Ella, being Libby's best friend, was well aware of her two great loves; cake and fashion.

"But that's not the only thing Ell," Libby croaked nervously. "I invited his new girlfriend too."

"WHAT!" Ella cried. "Libby Catherine Crosley you don't help yourself do you?"

"I know, I know," Libby giggled. "I'm an idiot. I'm so nervous. I just had to make this party harder for myself. Honestly Ella, I'm a wreck. I don't want to see him and least of all *her*, and even least of all at my *own party*!"

Ella sighed. Libby was indeed her own worst enemy; ever since they were little, Libby had always been getting herself, *and Ella*, into trouble.

"Oh Libs. Okay, you need to go and have a bath to relax. You have a few hours before the party and your mum is there to help too. I can come early if you like?"

"Hmm, don't worry about coming early but –"

"But the most important thing to do is to find a cracking outfit." There it was. Fashion. The key to Libby's heart. Libby worked as a stylist to the stars and her life was steeped in all things fashion. If Ella could distract Libby with clothes, accessories and make-up, then she might calm down.

"Oooh you're right Ell! Okay, what should I wear? I don't have that many dresses at my parents' house. But I've got a new Valentino number I haven't shown you yet – it's red, very Christmassy! Actually it might be a little over the top. I don't want to look desperate or have my dad's friends staring at my cleavage for a creepy amount of time; I don't want them dribbling as I pass around the appetizers!"

Ella grinned. "Libs, do you know you're wicked? What are your other options?" she asked as she looked at the Christmas roulades. She asked the lady behind the bakery counter how much the one with the white snowflake icing was, while Libby rummaged through her wardrobe on the other end of the phone.

Ella could hear the metallic screeching of the hangers as Libby rifled through mountains of clothes.

"Aha!" she squealed. "I've got that gorgeous black Versace dress?"

"Hmm, which one is that Libs?" Ella asked, confused by her friend's endless collection of couture.

"It's the velvety one. It's a bit old but it still fits."

"Oh that one! Definitely wear that!"

"Are you sure?" Libby asked hesitantly. Ella could tell she needed some more coaxing. She picked up the roulade from the counter and said "Definitely! I remember your arse looking particularly insane in that. Wear the Versace, you'll look fit to fuck."

Just as the reassuring words slipped out of her mouth, Ella turned around to see the Brown Haired man standing right in front of her. She almost dropped the roulade on the floor.

Shit, shit, shit! Her cheeks coloured from icy white to fiery red in seconds. *How embarrassing!* He stared at her with an unreadable expression. This second unexpected run in was not nearly as nice as the first one.

Ella could hear Libby's chuckle echoing menacingly through her phone speaker.

"Oh darling, thank you. You've cheered me up! I'm going to go and get ready now, got a million and one things to do before the party. I'll see you at eight, on the dot! Love you."

"See you tonight," Ella murmured quietly. She hung up her phone shyly and put it in her pocket. To her disappointment, the Brown Haired man recoiled from her with a faint attempt at a smile. Taking a few steps backwards, he turned and disappeared along with his basket. Ella was so angry at herself.

I can't believe he heard me say that! I was just trying to make Libby feel better!

But Ella's exasperation soon turned to chuckling. She barely knew the difference between Valentino and Versace; she wasn't good with brands, so it was ironic that this man had just been scared off by her fashion conscious slur.

He probably thinks I'm some stuck up designer whore... Ella shook the thoughts of self-doubt and embarrassment from her head; what did it matter what he thought about her anyway? She would never see him again.

On that note, Ella charged to the check out, paid for her items and left for home.

Chapter Two

Ella dunked her little toe into the bubbly water. It was too hot to submerge herself just yet, so she turned to the cupboards under the sink and rummaged around until she found a long mauve candle. She placed it in a candle holder on the side of the bath, lit it and waited for the lavender scent to fill the room. Killing time in order to let the bath cool, she walked out of her bathroom, across the open plan studio to the bookshelf where she kept her DVDs and CDs. Ella adored classic films, especially those set at Christmas. On the shelf stood *White Christmas* and *Holiday Inn*, which she had watched a silly amount of times.

Fred Astaire and Bing Crosby. *What gentleman they were. They knew how to romance a woman. They cannot leave me.* Ella lingered over the DVDs and moved on to her CD collection. She picked up a compilation CD named *Best Christmas Songs of All Time*, opened the case and placed the CD in her audio system that was built into the bottom shelf of the case. She knew CDs were outdated but the speakers in her old stereo were so good she couldn't resist using them still. She pressed play and the familiar opening chimes of 'All I want for Christmas is You' trickled out of the speakers.

She treaded the dark wooden floorboards back to the bathroom, dancing to the festive tune as she went. She kept the glass sliding door to her bathroom ajar so she could hear the music and untied her dressing gown.

The water was still boiling. Ella slowly lowered herself down past the bubbles and into the water as if going slower would make the water cooler. She screwed up her face and tensed her abs as she submerged her stomach and then her shoulders as she reclined. She finally plucked up the courage to dunk her head and when she came back up again to the sounds of Mariah Carey belting out the high notes, the soapy water lapped against the edge of the bath-tub and spilt over the edge. Ella took the sponge in front of her and washed herself while humming along to the song. She used the sponge as a microphone once she had finished washing.

"All I want for Christmas iiiiisss…youuuu ooooo!" Ella strained to reach the final top note but she didn't let her awful singing prowess stop her. She thrashed around in the hot water and bobbed her head to the fading beat like a chicken lacking rhythm. She squeezed a large dollop of shampoo out of the bottle and started massaging it into her scalp, creating a thick lather. She got a bit of foam in her ear that muted her hearing for a moment. When she used a towel to wipe out the shampoo, she heard the next track from the album spilling through the living room. Wham!'s 'Last Christmas' was jingling festively.

Last Christmas I gave you my heart but the very next day you gave it away.

Ella's stomach churned. She put down the towel and sat back against the wall of the bath, clasping the edges of the tub with her hands.

This song was about her. One of her favourite Christmas songs was now ruined by the memory of her ex-boyfriend! She hadn't heard it yet this year but of course it was going to upset her, she thought. Last Christmas she was with Robbie and he had literally given her heart away the very next day. Well the week after, but the lyrics tore through her just as hard, as if the song had been written to mock her.

Ella sighed as she leant against the cold tiles, her hair still covered in a white halo of bubbles. The depressing chorus persisted: *Last Christmas I gave you my heart but the very next day you gave it away.* What had she been doing this time last Christmas, on the 15th of December?

She'd been waiting for Robbie at Fortnum and Mason to do their shop of opulent goodies for the festive season. It was one of their annual traditions but last year Ella had stood waiting for him for ages in the biting cold. After an hour she admitted defeat and went into the shop alone, half-frozen. He was clearly not coming to join her. As she had started to peruse the food court her phone had pinged and she read a message from Robbie: *Sorry Ell, working late again today. See you at home x*.

Working late, again! He had been so busy with work at the time that Ella felt like she had hardly seen him. Looking back, it was so obvious that something more had been going on, that it wasn't just work that was occupying his thoughts. But Ella didn't know that then and his suspicious behaviour had only proved to raise Ella's hopes of a Christmas proposal.

Her friends had all been hinting at it – Ella and Robbie had been together for six years, they were of the right age, they loved each other; it all seemed right, perfect even. Perhaps he was ring shopping and that was why he couldn't make it to Fortnum and Mason, she had thought. He was finalising the ring! Ella vowed not to chastise him for working late and let the next week run its natural course.

A few times that week she had cheekily alluded to rings and marriage, thinking that she was hot on the scent.

Then on Christmas Eve in their house in Chelsea, which spread over three floors, Ella believed the moment had finally arrived. It was after dinner, when they sat underneath the over-decorated Christmas tree to open an early present, a tradition Ella's father had started, that she believed Robbie was about to propose. Robbie fished through the pile of presents to reveal a small jewelry box that almost brought a tear to Ella's eye. Robbie normally had the cheekiest grin on his face when he watched her open presents but he didn't today.

This is the moment, Ella had thought as Robbie had pecked her on the cheek and passed her the box.

"Here you go darling," he said with a lack of enthusiasm.

But Ella was too excited to notice her boyfriend's indifferent expression.

She propped herself up so she was sitting on her knees, brushed the hair from her eyes and opened the box in apprehension.

"Oh."

It was a beautiful and delicate silver bracelet studded with sapphires and diamonds coiled up in a spiral so that it fit in the small box.

It was incredibly special but it wasn't a ring. Ella's hopes were dashed and Robbie could see the look of surprise on her face.

"What's wrong Ell? Don't you like it?"

"No, no, I do," she said forcing a smile. "It's lovely."

She was distraught. She had built up this moment throughout the day and dinner and when she saw the right shaped box she felt certain Robbie was going to propose.

Robbie got up to clean the dishes and didn't say another word until they went to bed.

What is up with him at the moment? she had thought.

Ella entertained the idea that perhaps the bracelet in the small box was just a joke at her expense which was leading up to the real proposal? Perhaps he had chosen the small box on purpose to frustrate her and he was really going to propose to her on Christmas Day when his whole family was there? That sounded more like Robbie. Showing off to as many people as possible – that's how he'd do it. And he loved to wind her up. Yes, this was all just a game to throw her off the trail! Ella perked herself up and had gone bed that night sure that Robbie would propose the next day. She fell asleep looking at the sapphires and diamonds in the bracelet on her bedside table, the precious stones glimmering with hope.

But the next day, there was no ring to match the beautiful bracelet. They opened their stockings and presents in muted mirth and had a lovely, but normal, Christmas Day at his parents' grand house in Kensington.

Ella, disappointed and angry at herself for letting her friends' gossip raise her hopes, decided to let life slip back to the usual after the holidays. Robbie would propose when he was ready and in the meantime she would support him while work was stressful.

She said nothing as Robbie spent every day of the following week in the office even though he had booked it off as holiday. He would get back at eleven o'clock and slip into bed with Ella, cuddle her and say nothing. She nuzzled into him, hoping she could dispel his stress with kisses, replacing words with affection because she didn't know what to say to him when he wouldn't let her in.

But all her worries were replaced with new, bigger ones on New Year's Eve. When Ella got back to the Chelsea flat after seeing Libby for a coffee, she had found a note waiting for her on the kitchen table.

My darling Ell,

I've taken the job in Chicago that we talked about a few months ago. I'm leaving tonight. I think we both know it hasn't been right recently. We've had the most amazing six years but I'm not ready for the commitment you want. I don't want to disappoint you, you're too good for that and deserve more than me. You deserve better. You will always be the most incredible woman I'll ever have had the pleasure of meeting. But I don't think I can ever commit to marriage. I know how much it means to you. You spoke of it recently and it panicked me. I'm sorry. Please forgive me. I think you'll be happier this way.

Robbie x

Ella's heart dropped. She felt like her whole body had just been torn in half by a chain saw. She couldn't process the blurry words on the page and she read it over and over again until it's contents and the scrawled handwriting were etched into her vision permanently. She could recite it word for word even now, a year on.

Ella, overwhelmed by despair, had collapsed on the floor in a heap. She had called Libby and sobbed down the phone, trying to explain what had happened. Libby cancelled her New Year's Eve plans and went straight to be at the side of her heart-broken best friend.

That night was the worst night of Ella's life. She felt hopeless, rejected, cast aside. All the love she had shown Robbie, all the years they had spent building their life together, he had just thrown away in a fit of panic. How carelessly he had done it. He had left her a note, a scrap of paper that became heavier and heavier every time she read it.

Ella didn't hear from him for weeks and those weeks turned into months. She told herself she was better off without him and convinced herself that everything she had once loved about him was irritating and repulsive.

He was too patronising. He was too argumentative. He was ostentacious. He was showy and image conscious. He was pedantic about the most annoying things, he was sexist, he was … he was everything bad in the world.

Ella heard the scratching of her CD in the player. She had been so lost in thought she hadn't realised that the machine was stuck on the same line, repeating eerily the same refrain again and again.

Now I know what a fool I've been, but if you kissed me now I know you'd fool me again. Chug chug chug. *Now I know what a fool I've been, but if you kissed me now I know you'd fool me again.* Chug chug chug. *Now I know what a fool I've been, but if you kissed me now I know you'd fool me again.*

The music blasted out truth and made her think of his kisses.

Oh his kisses. She sighed, finally submerging in the water to rinse out the shampoo that had almost set on top of her head. If he was here now, even after all the pain and heartbreak he had put her through, she knew she'd give in to his charm. She would melt at the touch of his hand. She'd be a fool again because he was so handsome, funny and sexy.

Ella sat up and wiped the water from her eyes. She moved onto the rose-infused conditioner and massaged it into her scalp while she thought about Robbie's redeeming features and ignored the squeaky repetition of Wham!'s Christmas classic. Robbie was hilarious, successful and ambitious. He was so seductive and incomparable in the bedroom …

Ella remembered the Christmas Eve that Robbie had whisked her off to Switzerland for a skiing holiday. They had spent the week in a five star hotel and having decided it was too cold outside to ski, even when they had piled on all their clothes, they spent the week in the hotel room without any clothes …

Ella was becoming aroused just thinking about her and Robbie's sensual holiday but she realised that she was back-tracking and forced herself to think of Robbie's faults. She dunked her hair in the hot water in order to cool off and rinsed out the conditioner.

She had to remember how furiously and often they had argued, how uncontrollably jealous and patronising he had been. Just because he spoke five languages and was exceptionally well-read, didn't mean he was better than everybody else.

Ella convinced herself that she was only thinking about him now because she had so many Christmas memories with him, it wasn't because she missed him. She vowed not think of him again that evening and stood up to drain the water from her body. Ella took out the plug, squeezed the excess water from her wild curls and stepped out of the bath. She had to stop that awful song.

Chapter Three

Ella stepped out of her car onto the frozen gravel and wrapped her scarf a little tighter. She was wearing a soft black poloneck with a denim dungaree dress over the top. The dress was cut into her waist, showing off her curves and although it was short with her tanned heeled boots, she wore thick black tights to make the outfit a bit more conservative. She looked over at the Crosley's family home. It was a beautiful cream farmhouse with a thatched roof and a duck-egg blue door. Hanging in the middle of the door was a decadent wreath, decorated with diagonally sloped red ribbons, white glossy pearls and fluffy old man's beard. Either side of the door were two pillars made from wooden beams. Misteltoe had been diligently wrapped around each pillar and it looked wonderfully festive. Ella walked down the gravel drive and onto the path that led to the front door. All the plants in the flowerbeds either side of the path were covered in a glittering film of horst frost which twinkled as she passed.

As Ella stepped onto the path, she took a deep breath and thought about what state Libby might be in with the imminent arrival of her ex-boyfriend, Marcus. She could see that the house was full of guests already; the glow of old antique lamps inside illuminated the shapes of marshmallow-sized Christmas coats and the light buzz of jingly Christmas music escaped the cracks of the old and drafty windows.

Ella was just about to reach the last step on the path when she lost her footing. Her left boot slipped on the frosty edge of the stone and as her body fell from underneath her, she felt panic surge through her body. Ella attempted to shift her body forward, hoping to grasp onto the left hand beam and grab at the mistletoe twines in front of her to steady herself, but as she lurched forwards, her right foot slipped too. After a wobbly dance on the ice, which even Michael Flatley would have been proud of, Ella fell. She closed her eyes ready to embrace the fall, hoping that the temporary darkness could numb the pain.

But the fall never came. She felt pressure on her right arm, a squeeze around her bicep and a hand placed on her left hip. Someone had caught her. She looked up, with strands of hair across her face, into the blue eyes of the Brown Haired man. Electricity ran through her; she knew this face. It was the stranger from the supermarket. He loosened his grip on her arm but kept his arms on her shoulders so she had a moment to steady herself. Ella blew the hair from off her face and took a step back from him.

"Th-thank you," she whispered. Regaining her composure, she straightened the edge of her denim hem and said in a louder, more confident voice: "I think I saw you earlier in Waitrose."

The man stared at her so intensely that it made Ella feel nervous.

"That could have been a disastrous fall," he replied finally. This was the first time that Ella had heard him speak. He was incredibly well-spoken but his voice had a touch of coarseness to it as if he had been a smoker or heavy drinker all his life. He was wearing the same brown suede jacket he had been wearing in Waitrose and somehow, he seemed more attractive now, perhaps because of the faint whiffs of his musty cologne Ella smelt on the bitter wind.

James Dean. That was who he reminded her of. He looked just like a brunette version of James Dean with his slightly quaffed hair, rusty stubble and enchanting eyes which were set back above light puffy bags. He even had the full seductive James Dean lips that looked like they should be hosting a Lucky Strike cigarette.

Ella realised she hadn't replied to him and had been staring hopelessly into his eyes.

Say something you idiot!

"Yes it could have been. I should have been more careful on the ice."

I should have been more careful on the ice? That's hardly exciting. Think, Ella.

Ella felt intimidated by the way the Brown Haired man stared at her.

Aware that this was the third time that day that she had stood in silence opposite this stranger making a fool of herself, Ella decided to throw herself into the situation and introduce herself.

"I'm Ella, Ella Moore." She smacked red lipstick-covered lips together and narrowed her eyes, waiting for the reply from this man. He took a step closer to her and as he spoke, she could see his breath on the air.

"I am Fergus, Fergus Lamb."

So the Brown Haired man is called Fergus and he seems to be mocking the way I introduced myself. Great start, Ella, Ella Moore..

Ella wanted to strike up a normal conversation with him but all she could think about was how her body felt after he had touched her arm. Just as Fergus started to raise his hand and speak again, the front door burst open in front of them.

"There you are! I thought I saw you from the window!" Libby was panting excitedly and Ella could see from the twinkle in her eye that she was a little drunk.

"Come in now, both of you. It's freezing out here. I see you've met already and I don't need to bother with introductions." Libby kissed both of them on each cheek and then proceeded to bark her orders.

"Ell, I need you. Fergus, Toby's in the kitchen!"

Fergus nodded and gestured to Ella to follow Libby through the front door first. Ella walked over the threshold, her cheeks now blushing after the abrupt interruption and stopped in the hallway. As Libby closed the door behind them, Fergus brushed past Ella. As he did so, he lightly placed his hand on her hip so that he could pass through the narrow hallway and into the kitchen without bumping into her. Her skin tingled. She watched him go and thought about what Libby had just said.

So Fergus is a friend of Libby's brother, Toby?

Ella turned to Libby who was shaking her mane of golden hair from side to side trying to add volume to it.

"How has it been so far? Is he here?" Ella asked.

"Yes, and the new girlfriend Jessica is *so* beautiful and *so* frickin' nice, I can't actually hate the bloody girl."

Ella chuckled. "Oh Libby, it's always hard seeing your ex with someone new. At least you look incredible." Libby was dressed in a short black velvet dress that showed off her long legs. Libby had sun-kissed skin all year round and adorable freckles which clustered around her nose. She flashed Ella a smile with her naturally red lips.

"Thanks darling!"

"Pleasure. Now I know you don't want to like her, but it will be much easier for you if she is nice." Libby frowned but Ella continued. "You and

Marcus were best friends for years before you dated and your families are good friends, so you want to keep a great friendship with him. If he is happy with someone who is genuinely nice then you can all be friends."

"Eugh, I guess you're right Ell."

"And it must have taken real guts for her to come here and meet all his friends and his stunning ex-girlfriend at her house; I admire her. Also, Marcus must have told her how important you are to him if she has agreed to coming here and walking straight into the lion's den!"

"Haha. I guess she is pretty brave to come here. She's also not really a threat because Marcus and I left it on good terms and we broke up because we grew apart not because one of us hurt each other. But it will just take time to get used to seeing him with someone else." Libby paused to think. "As much as I want to despise her, she really is lovely! She's a microbiologist or something sickeningly clever! Ha! I just hope she's good enough for him," she smirked.

"Haha, that's the spirit Libs! Could you imagine if she *was* a real terror? It would ruin your friendship and be a disaster. Now, introduce me to her and give me some of your Champagne."

Libby was in a brighter mood as she linked arms with her best friend and reentered the party. As soon as Ella stepped into the kitchen she was hit by the familiar smell of mulled wine. The room was filled with clusters of overexcited people, the clinking of glasses and wafts of cinnamon. The two girls sauntered to the kitchen table dodging festively plump individuals who stood in their paths. They poured themselves a drink and toasted to new beginnings. Ella spotted Libby's mother standing by the Aga and gestured to Libby she was going to say hello. Libby nodded and moved off to greet new guests arriving at the front door.

Elisabeth Crosley was an exceedingly glamorous woman who oozed charm. She was larger than life with enormous golden tresses, a huge bosom and long spidery eyelashes. Libby was a clone of her mother. Elisabeth Crosley had a soft spot for Ella and had taken her under her wing since her parents passed away, since they had been Elisabeth's oldest friends.

"Darling, hello! I am so glad you are here. I can see you've already lifted Liberty's spirits – well done! It's more than I can do. Honestly, she's been sulking all day."

Ella smiled and kissed Elisabeth on each cheek.

"Well I'm glad I was able to cheer Libby up a little. She was even able to praise the new girlfriend; she's quite accomplished apparently," Ella said.

"Quite right my lovely. Apparently, she's a quantum physicist or something. So long as she's good enough for him."

Ella chuckled at how similar Libby and Elisabeth were. She wondered if Jessica was a microbiologist or quantum physicist or if both the Crosley women's penchant for exaggeration had exceeded itself.

"Ella, have you seen my husband yet? Where *is* he?" Elisabeth asked wobbling her head as she always did when she talked.

"He's probably ignoring all our guests." Just as Elisabeth finished her sentence, William Crosley appeared at the other end of the kitchen in a green v-neck cashmere jumper and brown corduroys.

"William! Come here and help me, you keep running off!" Mrs Crosley echoed down the kitchen in her high-pitched authoritative voice.

William was a small man. He was much smaller than his wife who he was completely in awe of. He had rather large ears, red cheeks and rare royal blue eyes with fantastic streaks of light blue marbled through them. Ella could see that William must have been a handsome man in his youth.

"Oh hello Ella. It's lovely to see you. How are you?" William croaked as he hugged her.

"I am fine, thank you William. And you?" William adored Ella every bit as much as his wife did and he thought that she was a good influence on his fashion-conscious-party-attending rebel of a daughter.

"Wonderful thank you, but I'm afraid I can't chat now. Elisabeth is just about to tell me to fetch some fire wood from the stables, so I shall go!" William threw his hands up in the air comically in mock exasperation and grinned cheekily at his wife before shuffling off to perform his unspoken orders. She smiled back and turned to Ella.

"I must go and see to the guests. Keep your drink topped up and do go on down into the drawing room. I think the younger contingent are in there."

"Thank you Elisabeth. I have some puddings I brought for you but I left them in the car. I'll bring them in later," Ella said.

"Oh you needn't have my child! But thank you. You are staying here tonight? And you're coming to us on Christmas Day?" she asked as she walked off into the throng of the party.

Ella nodded enthusiastically and leant back against the Aga. She recognized most people in the room but she was most anxious to say hello to her school friends. Harry Pomeroy, Lara Allsopp and Charlie Bellamy, Ella and Libby's closest friends from school, were all crowded around the fridge at the other end of the kitchen. Ella stood up straight and went over to them.

"Ella!" cried Lara. There was a cacophony of *hellos* and *how are yous* as Ella greeted her friends.

"How are you Ell?" asked Charlie. "Did you just drive down from London?"

Charlie Bellamy was exceeding tall and had to crouch down to fit into the Crosley's low-ceiling kitchen. The Crosley's old country house was an obstacle course for the not so vertically challenged people of the party. The taller contingent had to watch out for the lethal beams that often appeared out of nowhere.

"Yes, I did. Don't tell me you just did too?"

"Yes! Oh we could have come down together and I could have driven you back tomorrow morning," Charlie replied as he put his arm affectionately around Ella's shoulder. Charlie was so tall, Ella always enjoyed leaning into her old friend. There was something so comforting and safe about him.

"Oh are you all staying the night too?" she asked as she squeezed Charlie's hand around her neck in a friendly way.

As all her friends nodded and started firing questions about how they were each spending their holidays, Fergus passed by in front of Ella. Ella saw him looking at Charlie's arm around her neck as he went over to the table to fill up his drink. Neither one of them broke their stare until he brought the glass up to his lips, tilted his head back to down his glass of champagne and filled it up once more.

"Isn't that right eh Ella?" Charlie joked as he pulled her in closer to his chest.

"Huh?" she said distractedly turning back to face her friends.

"Your New Year's Eve party is themed," Harry confirmed in his low unassuming voice.

"Oh yes, yes it is themed. Arabian Nights. It'll bring some warmth to London! Don't forget. You don't want to be running around London trying to pull a belly dancing costume together in that awfully miserable time between Christmas and New Year. I hate those days after Boxing Day, don't you?" Ella asked.

"Absolutely, *they're* so dreary. I'm *going as* Jasmine obviously. What are *you* going *as*?" Lara had a peculiar tendency to emphasize all the wrong words in a sentence. Ella thought it must stem from the time Lara had spent floating in and out of different international schools in her early teens as her parents jobs had taken them across the globe. It took a while to get used to but it was endearing.

The boys started to discuss how much they disdained fancy dress just as Ella pulled herself from out of Charlie's heavy grip. Flustered, she moved towards Lara.

"I'm so hot, are you? It's like an oven in here," Ella complained.

"*I* know. It so hot *because* there are *so* many people in here and because the *Aga's* on. And Beth keeps insisting *William* tops up the fire *in* the drawing room with *logs* every *three* minutes!" The two girls chuckled and commented on William's devotion to his wife. Elisabeth was clearly the boss of the Crosley household but everybody knew that William secretly loved being told what to do after years of commanding others in the Army.

"Have you *met* Jessica yet?" Lara asked changing the subject. "She's my new best *friend*! I need *to* go and tell her *the* name of my brother's company. We were talking about it *earlier* as they are both in the *same* field; I forgot earlier but I've remembered *now*. Come *through* with me," Lara said as she moved towards the drawing room.

Turning to Harry and Charlie, Ella said, "Boys I must go and say hello to Toby and Emily." She picked up a few entrees from the table, filled up her glass and followed Lara into the drawing room hoping to find Toby and his pregnant wife. She spotted them on a scarlet sofa in the corner of the large drawing room and sat down next to them.

Ella hadn't seen Toby since he had come back from his latest tour in Afghanistan and she hadn't seen Emily since she had fallen pregnant; after such a long time they had lots to talk about and they somehow managed to condense a year's worth of gossip, war anecdotes, painting disasters and baby anxieties into a lively twenty minute chat. Ella learnt that they were having a girl and she was due on Christmas Day. Toby and Emily were oscillating between the name Holly or Ivy for the yuletide baby.

Ella couldn't help but think that it was a bit quaint to give the child such an obviously festive name but she soon realised she was being too cynical and that actually, both names were lovely. She welcomed a new glass of champagne that was presented to her on an ornate silver tray by one of the waiters that the Crosley's had hired for the party.

"Ivy." She tested out the name, with her head tilted in deliberation. "*Ivy*. I think you should name her Ivy; it's more rare and somehow more feminine. And less linked to Christmas, I think." Ella couldn't help but add the last bit. Emily began to nod in agreement when Charlie and Harry joined them at the sofa. Ella tried to squeeze up but with the heavily pregnant Emily and broad muscular Toby, there wasn't room for all five of them on the sofa. She stood up and offered the boys the place which they took, but not without pulling Ella down onto their laps.

"Oh Harry, Charlie, I can stand!" Ella protested as she tried to force her way to her feet.

"No," Charlie said cheekily. "If there's no room for us on the sofa, there's no room for you to stand!"

Ella rolled her eyes and pouted at the boys in feigned anger. She shifted herself over to Charlie's lap so she could lean against the arm of the sofa for support. The conversation darted between the Migrant Crisis, *Strictly Come Dancing* and the quality of snow in Val-d'Isère this season as the waiters brought them trays and trays of hors d'oeurves. Ella observed that Emily was having some strong pregnancy cravings as she looked ready to gag when the salmon entrees were wafted around, but greedily grabbed a whole platter of the cocktail sausages when they were passed her way. She balanced the large tray on her lap which made the sofa seem even smaller.

Ella was starting to feel the effects of the champagne she had been drinking. She had hardly been at the party an hour but had managed to drink four glasses already. She couldn't tell if it was just the alcohol she had consumed or if it was also the room, but she was incredibly hot.

She stood up, excused herself and went to the large window at the back of the drawing room. She took it off the latch and opened it. It was a large bay window with a cushion built into it. She opened the window even wider and sat as close to the frame as she could with her cheek touching the cold glass. Once she had cooled down, Ella surveyed the room. She could see the beautiful Spencers, the rather dull Posenbys, the wild Cuthberts, the apologetic Brandons and her favourite of them all, the infectiously happy Brewers. Then there was Charlie, Harry, Lara, Libby, Toby, Emily, Marcus and his girlfriend Jessica and Fergus ... he was talking to all of her friends and had taken her spot. He must have walked over just after she had left.

Does he not like me? she thought as she watched him. She crossed her legs and signaled to a waiter, asked for some sparking water and rested her hand on her chin.

Who is this man? He was incredibly well dressed yet he looked nothing like the people at this party. His suede jacket was out of place amongst all the pink coloured chinos and dusty blue blazers. He was wearing a black poloneck. Not only did he look like he didn't belonged at this party, but he looked like he didn't belong in this era. Ella looked at his deep brown hair and red-flecked silvery beard. She thought of James Dean again. A brunette James Dean ...

"He's called Fergus."

Mrs Crosley sat down next to Ella and the surprise and force of Mrs Crosley's voluptuous body meeting the cushion beside her almost made her spill her drink.

"Ohh he he he," she laughed. "I didn't mean to startle you Ella. It's just I thought I'd bring you a napkin. I could see you dribbling from the other side of the room."

Ella regained her composure, embarrassed that Elisabeth had caught her mid hypnosis. "Oh gosh, was I really that obvious? Subtlety has never been my strong point." She paused. "He's absolutely gorgeous."

"I know Ella. Sadly, I'm not looking for a lover right now – naturally he was very disappointed when I told him."

Mrs Crosley had a wicked wit.

"How do you know him? Is he a friend of Toby's? From school?" she inquired.

"Army friend, my dear."

"Really?" Ella replied, shocked that this delicate and artistic looking man could be the product of military training.

"Oh quite so. They are very good friends. Obviously, they are nothing like each other, but doesn't that make the best of friendships sometimes?"

Ella reflected upon what Elisabeth had said.

"Right, now it's time I introduced you! You will get on like a house on fire, I don't know why I haven't thought of it before!" Elisabeth exclaimed while getting up.

"Oh, we did meet earlier very briefly, so you don't need to introduce."

But Elisabeth was already at the sofa crammed full of Ella's friends. By the time Ella had got to the sofa, it seemed as if Elisabeth was giving a treatise on all Ella's merits. Elisabeth gestured to Ella introducing her to her best friends as if it was the first time they had all met her. She felt like her cheeks were reaching an unnatural shade of purple. Her alcohol consumption and the ungodly heat of the room were not helping her embarrassment dissipate.

"I've pulled her away from the window because we want her company! It's not a party without Ella around," Mrs Crosley said with a knowing smile and tilt of the head.

"Thanks Beth," Ella said with a slight hint of sarcasm.

"Well, we were just talking *about* the new exhibition *at* the V *and* A," Lara stated. "I *would* love to go but it seems no one *is* interested."

"I am," Fergus and Ella replied simultaneously.

There was a slight chuckle from the group and Ella felt like she was back in the school playground.

"Are you interested in art Ella?" Fergus asked. Aha! Here was a question she could answer, a chance for a proper conversation devoid of awkward silences, regrettable eavesdropping and clumsiness.

"Ye—"

"Of course she is! She's a painter," Mrs Crosley cried. Fergus' face lit up and Ella noticed.

"A marvelous one. I want to get her to do a family portrait of us but then that's not your type of art is it darling Ella?" Elisabeth's voice bellowed around the whole room and made Ella feel like she had to address the entire room's guests in return. She coughed slightly and paused briefly to reflect on the Crosley's love of volume.

"Yes, I'd happily paint you a family portrait but it wouldn't be any good and you'd be incredibly disappointed, because, as you say, I am not a portrait painter," Ella replied modestly with a smile. Elisabeth, distracted by the waiter and the new flavour of canapés he offered her, turned her attention from Ella.

Hoping that Fergus' slightly raised eyebrows were a show of his interest in art or *her* art, Ella addressed him alone.

"I am more of an abstract artist. I help run a gallery in London but I am also an artist too."

"Oh great. Have you always painted? What sort of thing to you paint?" Fergus asked coolly.

The rest of the group had resumed their own conversations and Fergus stepped closer to Ella at the edge of the sofa, waiting for her reply.

"Yes, I've always been a painter. I studied fine art at university and went on to work in advertising for a few years. But after realising it was not in the least bit satisfying, I took up painting professionally and plunged into the art world again. I mainly paint natural scenes but abstract stuff." *Abstract stuff? Did I really just say that? Years of studying art, its terminology and movements and all you can muster to describe your style is 'abstract stuff'.*

Fergus nodded with what looked like enthusiasm. Was he genuinely interested in art or was he feigning politeness? Ella wasn't sure but she continued anyway.

"I use oils on canvas and occasionally I work with clay and sculpt. Do you paint?" she asked.

"Oh no no. I would love to be able to draw but sadly I've never acquired the skill or the patience." His voice was hoarser than before, perhaps because he had had a few drinks since they had talked in the doorway. His sultry tones were so inviting.

"Ah I see. Not very creative then?"

"Well I am a photographer," he said, running his hands through his rich hair.

"Oh really?" Ella couldn't contain her surprise. "Amateur?"

"No. Professional."

"Oh," Ella said.

"Is that disappointing?" he asked grinning a little.

"Nooo not at all. It's just I thought you were in the Army – Elisabeth told me you met Toby in the Army."

"Well she isn't wrong. I did meet Toby in the Army. But I am a war photographer, a photo journalist. We were stationed at the same base – I was there to document while he was fighting. I've never had any military training." He had moved his hands from his hair and was now brushing a patch of his stubble under his chin.

47

"Ah, I see. That makes a little bit more sense. I didn't think you looked like you were in the Army." As soon as Ella had spoken she knew that her words had come out wrong. She hadn't meant to cause offense, but by the reaction on Fergus' face she saw that he wasn't going to let her remark slide. He leant back on the sofa as if to settle in to enjoy this moment. A devilish smile appeared on his face.

"Oh I don't look manly enough for the Army – is that what you mean? Not strong enough?" he teased.

"Oh gosh, that's not what I meant at all!" she said, placing her hand on his arm. "I just meant that you looked more artistic, a little more sensitive than that." Fergus' eyes dazzled with mischief. Ella gently pulled away her hand when she realised it was still lingering on his arm.

"Well you're right. I don't think there is anyone on earth more sensitive than a photographer." They both chuckled and took a sip of their champagne.

"I'd love to see some of your artwork," Fergus exclaimed boldly, breaking the moment of silence.

Then, as if from nowhere, Mrs Crosley appeared and said: "Well you can next week. She's having an exhibition in London. She's doing *so* well! You must come. You must – Ella Fitzgerald Moore, tell him he must!" She smiled at them both before leaving them alone again.

The pair laughed at Elisabeth's intrusion and Ella composed herself. "I was just about to say, if Elisabeth hadn't beaten me to it, that I have an exhibition next week and if you were free or had nothing else to do, then please come along. There will be cheap complimentary cava and stale nibbles by the bucket load if my artwork doesn't sell it."

"I would love to come." Fergus' eagerness shined through his words but he managed to maintain a level of smoothness, of utter coolness, that made Ella feel heady.

"Now I have two questions for you Ella ..." She nodded obligingly. "Firstly, does Mrs Crosley butt into every conversation you ever start?"

"Ah, yes! It seems so. I'm like her second daughter so she's probably less polite with me than you!"

"Ha ha. She's wonderful, the life and soul of the party."

"Absolutely. You might have already guessed, but she was a real party girl when she was younger, well so I'm told. A bit like —"

"Libby?" he asked.

"Quite. Much to William's dismay! Now what was your second question?"

"Ah. Well I was going to ask about your name. Elisabeth just called you Ella *Fitzgerald* Moore ... is that your middle name?"

Ella nodded. "It's not my middle name as such but it's an honourary one. My parent's named me Ella after the great singer and so I've sort of inherited the nickname *Fitzgerald*, which I'm fond of, or *Fitz* which I hate. It makes me sound like a stiff upper lip butler who is more obsessed with maintaining a hierarchal social order than his liberal master."

Fergus chuckled. He looked so irresistible when he smiled. For a moment, they stared at each other and said nothing. Ella couldn't believe that the beautiful man she had seen in Waitrose only this afternoon was now standing in front of her. What were the chances that he had been in the same supermarket in London and then at the same party all the way out in Kent? Ella turned to the sofa and saw Libby flash her a knowing smile and raise of the eyebrow. Ella understood perfectly what Libby was trying to insinuate and she ignored it totally.

The room had filled up since she had started talking with Fergus. It was brimming with Christmas joy; overly animated guests, perhaps a little too merry for their own good, were perching on the edge of coffee tables, leaning against the sofas, walls and against the grandmother clock. They were diligently informing their audiences of their Christmas plans and everybody was listening and nodding with enthusiasm. Ella overheard people's plans and hoped that some of hers would be more exciting than just ice-skating at Somerset

House and going to Winter Wonderland. There was nothing wrong with doing any of these things but for Londoners the novelty wore off after a while and it didn't help that she had gone to all of these places with Robbie.

This Christmas, she wanted to do something original, something different. She wanted to go to places she never would usually and she wanted to make new Christmas traditions and memories, ones Robbie wouldn't be part of.

Ella turned back to Fergus who was still looking at her with unparalled intensity. She couldn't help but feel that there was an air of excitement between them; an invisible ball of throbbing heat was floating somewhere between them, glowing and expanding with possibility and the unknown. Neither of them spoke again and the tension was unbearable.

"Do you smoke?" Fergus finally asked.

"For my sins," she replied with a glimmer of mischief in her eye.

"Would you like to go outside for a cigarette? It's absolutely boiling in here."

Chapter Four

Ella and Fergus stood on the patio at the back of the Crosley's farmhouse. They could hear the merriness of the guests escaping the cracks in the old house's crooks and crannies and they could feel the dampness in the air. The atmosphere felt heavy and wet as if it might rain, but it was turning colder by the second, which perhaps meant snow.

"That's better," Ella said as she pulled out a packet of cigarettes from the pocket in her denim dress. She leant on the garden table made of antique steel and padded down her body for a lighter. Fergus stepped towards her with a silver zippo in his hand.

"Allow me."

He flipped the cap off the lighter, exposing the light blue powerful flame and drew it towards Ella. Once the cigarette was lit, Fergus leant back against the table next to her.

She offered him one of her cigarettes, gesturing the packet towards him and raising her eyebrows. He shook his head.

"I quit," he said.

"Then why did you ask me outside for a cigarette?" Ella demanded flirtatiously.

"How else was I going to get you alone?" he asked, confidently drawing a little closer to her so that his face was only a foot away from hers. Ella's eyes flashed with surprise and excitement. *He's daring. Daring but sweet.*

She smirked and looked away shyly. She fiddled with the edge of her skirt but decided to looked back at him and flirt back with confidence. She propped her elbow on her hip cocquetishly as she breathed in and out on the cigarette.

She realised she hadn't said anything in reply to his cheeky question about getting her alone. Just as she was preparing to say something equally cheeky back, he asked her for a cigarette.

"No way," Ella replied playfully. "You've quit remember. And I won't be the one to tempt you." She dropped her cigarette on the floor, stubbed it out with the heel of her boot and put it in the edge of a nearby flowerpot, distinctly aware that he was watching her every move.

"Oh I think we're way past that," Fergus said responding to her playfulness. "I hope this is not the last time I'll be tempted by you …"

Ella didn't know where to look. Her breathing was quickening and she could feel her body sliding towards Fergus who was only inches away now. *He likes me. He likes me.*

Their faces were so close that their noses were almost touching. Ella could smell his alluring cologne and the sweetness of his breath. She wanted to kiss him but she was paralyzed by the acuteness of her desire for him. Fergus delicately placed his hand on her cheek, caressed her soft skin and lowered his gaze to her lips. He placed his thumb on her red lip, and focused on each centimeter of her skin as if it would be the last time he would ever see her face.

No man had ever looked at her like this before. Suddenly his lips were on hers, kissing her lightly but with such passion that her whole body tingled in response. She arched her back into him as she kissed him with more force, her tongue meeting his as he ran his hands wildly through her even wilder hair.

They parted, panting, overwhelmed by power of the kiss.

Fergus and Ella looked at each other, their heavy gazes acknowledging that something special had just occurred between them. Ella wiped the slight stain of red lipstick gently from the corner of Fergus's mouth and smiled. He took her hand and kissed it gently.

"I've wanted to kiss you from the moment I saw you in Waitrose."

"Me too," Ella said finding her voice, a little croaky after their tantalizing embrace. "But I thought you must have thought me rather silly after you heard my conversation and saw how clumsy I was at the door," she confessed.

"What conversation? The second time I saw you, when I came up to you again at the bakery counter, I saw you were on the phone the moment you turned around, but I didn't hear your conversation."

Ella was amazed. He hadn't heard her stupid comment about the Versace dress! Or was it Valentino? Ella didn't care and was so relieved that he hadn't heard her remark.

"I was just too nervous to ask you out. I had just about plucked up the courage to introduce myself when I saw you were on the phone still and I bottled it."

Ella laughed. "You were about to ask me out?"

"Yes!"

"Bloody Libby always interrupting."

"Like mother like daughter eh?"

"Uh huh." Ella smiled.

"Hey, what did you say on the phone that you were mortified that I might have heard?" Fergus asked inquisitively, drawing closer to her again.

"Oh nothing!" Ella said, taking the opportunity presented to hide the monstrous comment. "We should go inside now," she continued.

"Are you cold?" he asked her, gesturing thoughtfully at his jacket.

"No, I'm fine, thank you. I just think if we stay out here any longer we might have a busybody

Elisabeth on our hands, doing what she does best and I don't know about you, but I'd much rather we went in on our own accord."

Fergus chuckled and nodded in agreement. He stood up from the table and politely gestured for Ella to walk in first. She steadied herself, tried to shake off the tingly feeling that had spread through her entire body and walked towards the door, mulling over the delight of their kiss.

As they reached the back door, Fergus placed his right hand gently on her arm.

"Ella, excuse me if I'm being forward but would you like to go out with me sometime this week?"

Ella's mouth curled into a coy smile. Her nose wrinkled and she bit her lip while looking up to the sky in mock deliberation. "Yes," she said triumphantly.

*

Libby waved off the last of her guests and shut the front door to keep the biting cold away. She roamed into the kitchen and saw her friends dancing manically to 'Driving Home for Christmas' with various cleaning equipment in hand. Charlie was playing imaginary drums with some dishcloths, Harry was strumming the broom like the air guitar it was, Lara was wiggling her bottom while washing dishes in the sink and Ella was singing, clinging with one hand to a dustpan and brush that was serving nicely as a microphone. They were making an absolute racket, hitting all the wrong notes at all the wrong times and muddling up the lyrics. Libby observed her mad friends, grabbed a bin bag and joined in.

With all hands on deck, the cleaning had taken no time at all. Within half an hour, they were all sitting around the kitchen table with a bottle of red wine reminiscing about their school days. They talked of how they'd snuck behind the games shed to steal their first cigarette, the pranks they'd play on their teachers and the embarrassing people they'd dated. Elisabeth, William, Toby and Emily had retired for the evening but luckily their rooms were nowhere near the kitchen; they were at the other end of the house, a fact the young friends took full advantage of as they screeched and screamed at the top of their lungs.

The gang huddled around the table looking over a new game called Linkee that Harry had bought the Crosleys for Christmas. On each card you had to answer four questions and guess what the link was between all four answers. They played the game until Lara had won, with heated arguments and passionate disagreements colouring the hour. Charlie had got so hysterical at one point, claiming that he shouted the link first that he'd fallen off his chair and the others had burst into a raucous of laughter.

"No you did not!" Libby screeched. "You're a little liar Charlie, Lara absolutely shouted it first!"

"Okay," Charlie laughed. "You win, I'll be good."

"Ha *ha* victory!" Lara gloated. "I *told* you I'm the champion *of* these games – I always win *Trivial* Pursuit and this game is *a* breeze in comparison!"

"Alright, Miss 'I've got two degrees from Cambridge'! We all know you're a *genius*!" Libby said jokingly. "Is anyone hungry? I'm starving," she continued as she surveyed her tipsy friends. They all looked as if they could do with some food to sober them up.

There was a murmur of approval as Liberty rose to check the pantry for snacks. She came back empty handed.

"I don't know how but we're out of almost everything! This party has cleared our supplies. No cheese, sorry guys! Some host I am!"

"Oh, I forgot! Libby I brought some cakes for you, they are in the car. I'll go get them."

"Brilliant! Thanks Ell," Libby beamed. "You always save the day." She drew a bit closer to Ella and said more quietly, "Well you saved my day and calmed me down – thank you darling."

Ella smiled warmly back at her. "Anytime. Now who wants mince pies?" she asked the group.

"I'll go get them, it's freezing outside. Give me your keys Ell," Charlie said, moving to stand.

"Oh thanks Chaz. Here you go."

Whilst Charlie was going to fetch the puddings, Lara topped up their glasses and Harry fetched some plates and forks. Ella sat at the table and thought about what had happened a few hours ago outside on the patio. So much had happened in one day. The supermarket felt like days ago and she could hardly believe she had bumped into Fergus twice in one day in both the city and the country. And he was taking her on a date on Monday night. She wondered where he might take her, what they might be doing and what she should wear. Not one to usually worry about her clothes or the way she looked, she suddenly found herself feeling nervous about such a trifling thing. She had never felt nervous around a man before and she wondered why she did so with Fergus.

"Helooo. I said helooooo."

Ella was vaguely aware that someone near her was making noise. She pried her eyes off the stone floor and looked up to see four pairs of eyes staring at her.

"Earth to Ella!" Libby exclaimed.

She chuckled as she realised she had been daydreaming and hadn't heard a word of what her friends had said to her.

"Sorry, I was miles away," she said guilty with a shrug of her shoulders.

"Were you dreaming of lover boy?" Lara teased.

"I…I…don't be so absurd! I was thinking about what Christmas presents I still needed to buy," she said, knowing full well her friends would not believe her.

"Mmmhmm," Libby challenged.

"Oh shut up and pass me a fork!" she cried.

Chapter Five

Ella and Fergus were sat in the dark, metres apart from each other. The mad hatter was sitting in between them and the Queen of Hearts was cackling wildly in a corner. For their first date, Fergus had taken Ella to Alice's Adventures Underground, an interactive theatre evening. Far down the rabbit hole now, Ella and Fergus were being asked to choose whether they wanted to shrink or grow, drink or eat, and were on a quest to find Alice, who was missing.

Ella heard somebody move next to her and then suddenly the lights were flashing neon green and she could see the outline of Fergus' stubble and in the background a tunnel lined with pages from old books. She felt as if she was sinking into a parallel world, one full of magic and kaleidoscopic rivers of sounds and patterns.

Fergus' face was flickering in and out of focus as the strobe lights persisted. This was the most surreal tea party Ella had ever been to, the only tea party she had ever been to, come to think of it.

Fergus squeezed her hand and through the sporadic lighting, she could see a purple Cheshire cat grin projected onto the wall behind her. Ella had heard all the hype surrounding this night and had been meaning to get tickets. They had sold out too quickly for her to get her hands on any but luckily Fergus' friend was the manager for the venue and gave him a heads up when some tickets were returned.

The whole night had been filled with topsy-turvy colours, walls replaced with ceilings and ceilings swapped for floors. At one point, Ella had been taken off into a tiny room lined with a mosaic of mirrors by a gigantic lime-coloured caterpillar and been made to write a poem about her suit of cards, diamonds. It was all incredibly exciting in that half confused sort of way and Ella was having a blast, even if she didn't understand all the gimmicks of the evening.

After escaping their tunnel, Ella and Fergus were led into a grand courtroom where the 'hearts' were found guilty and where Tweedledum and Tweedledee performed a mesmerizing circus act. The pièce de résistance was a cascading waterfall of teacups and cocktails which all the guests could drink from and dance around as the theatrical experience morphed into a party with a live band that arose from the depths of a backdrop made to look like a pile of rubbish, a wasteland.

Ella and Fergus were lost in Wonderland and it was perfect.

As the experience drew to a close, the couple exited the venue that was dug deep down under

Waterloo station and walked over the Jubilee bridge to embankment.

"It's *so* nice when the hype is justified," said Ella. "So often, something like this is bigged up to enormous proportions and then it almost always falls short. It's so disappointing when that happens. But I thought that was great; tremendously fun and truly imaginative."

"I agree, it was so organic, not too overdone or micromanaged. I get the feeling that the experience is different every night because a different crowd comes in and participates and that's just as it should be. I honestly felt like I was a kid ambling through a magical land for most part of it. The set was magnificent!"

"It was wonderful, thank you." Ella smiled thinking about the sensational evening they had spent together.

"It was. I've really had a great time tonight," Fergus said, taking her hand in his. Holding hands, becoming one unit, the pair could take on the panicked robotic Christmas shoppers with more ease. These shoppers, each on their own sacred mission, scanning the urban landscape for their targets, straining to complete their hunt for the 'perfect' present, looked like automated players in a video game. They were human-sized Pac-Men, changing their programmed paths only when another shopper threatened to swallow them whole.

Ella looked past the stress of the street and saw the tinkling Christmas lights arching above them over Villiers Street. The minute orbs sparkled against the dark blue sky and acted as understudies for the true stars that were hidden by the London smog.

Fergus followed Ella's gaze up to the sky, leant in to her and whispered: "I would love to see you again this week." They had stopped outside embankment station and were facing each other now. "If you have time with your exhibition that is," he continued while adjusting his scarf, with a touch of nervousness.

"I would like that," she replied. "I've actually taken this week off work so I can prepare for the exhibition on Friday. I'll use the days to add finishing touches to the paintings and help dress up the Beat Gallery. Then hopefully I'll have the evenings to relax a bit."

"Oh cool. Well, are you free tomorrow night? If you're too busy, please just say but I think I've just thought of something really fun we could do."

"Okayy," she said suspiciously. "But only if you tell me what it is."

"Where would be the fun in that? It will be much better as a surprise, I promise you."

Fergus leant into Ella's face and pressed his nose against hers. He brushed her lips with his and began to kiss her again. She could feel warmth radiating between every part of their bodies that touched.

"I'll take that as a yes then," he whispered smugly.

Ella smirked, kissed him again and said, "Text me a time and a place."

*

Ella woke up the next morning with the sun on her eyes. Dappled sunlight lay lightly over her bed and on her floorboards, the pattern created by the sun peeping through slits in the heavy white blinds that covered her window. She rubbed the sleep out of her eyes and sat up. She switched on her blue Roberts radio and let the tinkering of Classic FM bring her calmly into the realm of the living. She yawned, stretched her arms high above her head and began to relive last night's kiss. When Fergus had swooped in and pressed his lips against hers she thought her legs were going to topple beneath her. As soon as she kissed him, everything, the street, the Christmas lights, the noise of the bustling shoppers, the heckles of the tramps and the tinkering of glasses from punters outside Gordon's Wine Bar had been totally obliterated. The kiss had swept her into a vacuum where only she and Fergus existed and it was only on opening her eyes again that she remembered where she had been, on Villiers Street, in London.

Ella crept out of bed and opened the blinds to let in the full force of the light. It was a crisp day with clear blue sky and frost on the ground. She walked over to the breakfast bar and put her coffee machine on.

Ella lived in an open plan studio in North London. Two years ago, an innovative architect had come across a large warehouse with roomy storerooms he thought could be converted into trendy urban studios; one year later, the building acted as a sort of artists' commune, one which Ella had fallen in love with straight away and moved into when Robbie left her. The warehouse was situated in a part of London which had previously been a hellhole of crime, littered with monstrous 1970s grey concrete blocks, but fortunately for Ella, was now being hailed as the new sanctuary and hang out for artists. It was up and coming and the price of the studio reflected that; the value of the flats in the block had raised astronomically and she was glad to be sitting on what would one day be a tidy investment.

But regardless of price or location, Ella loved the openness of the room and that she had been able to buy it and furnish it entirely by herself. It had been a blank canvas for her to play with and although it looked like a dump from the outside, when you slid the green metallic warehouse door open you entered into a cave of treasures. A tall grey wall divided the room into two sections; her living space on the left and her work space on the right. The wall acted as a bedhead for her double bed that was covered in cream and charcoal coloured soft cushions. In the living area a window which ran from floor to ceiling was positioned on the back wall. On the left of the window stood Ella's bookshelf, on which a collection of globes sat. To the left of that, was her bathroom, the only part of the flat which was sectioned off with a nifty sliding glass door that Ella had painted herself in light blues and turquoises, like a stained glass window. Then opposite her bed was the kitchen area, which had an island that functioned as a breakfast bar with two tall steel stools.

Ella brushed her teeth and returned to the kitchen where her coffee was now ready. It was just past nine o'clock and she had a busy day ahead of her. Yesterday she had decided which of her last pieces should go into the exhibition. She was showcasing twenty paintings in her first exhibition called "Elementary Natures". The collection was a series of perspectives on the most basic elements; fire, water, earth and wind and looked to explore stock times of day; sunrise, sunset, dusk, dawn and twilight. Ella hoped that the collection captured her interpretations of the mood and atmosphere of these times of day through different landscapes.

The paintings were going to be transported to the gallery on Thursday so if she wanted to make any final changes to them she had to do it today or tomorrow. She had to allow ample time for the paintings to dry before they were moved.

Ella took her coffee through to her working studio behind the dividing wall at the head of her bed. She put on all her side lamps to illuminate the paintings and wondered around thinking over any changes that needed to be made. Her artist's studio was the same size as her living area. Luckily, Ella had bought a ground floor flat that had incredibly high ceilings; the sliding metallic door of her studio was large enough to fit even her biggest canvas that was some 15ft tall and 10ft wide.

As Ella looked at her paintings, she couldn't shake the images of Alice's Wonderland from her head. The colours of the caterpillar that had led her to a mirrored cupboard to write a poem for the Queen of Hearts had inspired her greatly. She felt now that her green oil painting entitled 'Noon Grass' needed more green. It needed some of the brilliant flicks of luminescent lime she had experienced last night – they would make it brighter and bolder so that the curves of the canvas were highlighted and the painting looked more 3D. Ella put her coffee down on the large oak desk she used to mix colours and started to sift through her brushes. She found the right one, a coarse, thick one and reached for a new colour she had mixed up only a few days ago.

Ella hand made all her own paints, mixing coloured pigments with oil to create the exact shade she desired. This florescent green she had made recently was left over paint she had made for a friend who bought her colours from Ella. But now, inspired by her trip with Alice, Ella was going to use it herself. She dipped her brush into the slimy looking green that she called *Lime Light* and started to blend it in with the darker green arcs already existing on the canvas.

Over the course of the day, Ella went on to alter three different paintings; to 'Toasted Sunset' she added an extra blood-orange paint to some of the lines of light rebounding off the horizon. She called this paint *Moroccan Fire* and used her fingertips to add texture to the oils. She also added tiny strips of gauze to the edge of the sun that she had painted with her favourite colour *Burnt Sienna*.

Ella moved on to 'Midnight Water' and used the opposite end of her paintbrush so it acted like a pencil and she began to lightly etch the words "flow" and "drip" into a deep purple section of the canvas. As the previous paint was dried, bits of the hardened paint crumbled away and added another dimension to 'Midnight Water'. The tunnel last night that had been plastered in book pages had inspired her to add these words to the painting. When her and Fergus had been in the tunnel, Ella had felt like they had gone underwater as the sound of their voices was muted and a bubbling sound of pipes and steam had been produced. Ella wanted to recreate that sense of fluidity she had experienced so she added *dripflowdripflowdrip* to one of the main arcs of the sea in 'Midnight Water'.

To her largest canvas, 'Sunrise Sun' she added gelatinous flicks of fiery yellow to the far right hand quarter of the canvas. She wanted to add the flicks vertically so she stood at the opposite end of her studio and launched *Scorched Mustard* in the air, her arms swinging in an arched motion as if she was ringing church bells. Because of techniques like this Ella's studio floor, ceiling and walls were covered in specs of multi-coloured paint. It looked like a bag of skittles had exploded into the room.

Ella stood back to observe the changes she had made to her paintings when she heard her phone bleep in her room.

Oh shit, what time is it? Ella rushed to the sink in the corner of her art studio, scrubbed her hands and used a bit of white spirit to get off the more stubborn paint. She dried her hands and she rushed to her phone. It was six forty-five and she had completely lost track of time being so absorbed in her painting.

The message had been from Libby: *Tell me about your hot date last night! Still on for lunch tomorrow? X*

And she had another from Fergus from this morning at 11.13am which she hadn't heard: *Greenwich station, 8.00pm.*

Ella had to move fast if she was going to be ready in time; she was still in her pyjamas, she hadn't thought about what she was going to wear and she had to cross the whole of London to get to Greenwich. Greenwich. What was he taking her to do? After last night, she knew it was going to be something interesting and off the wall. But all she knew about Greenwich was that the Royal Observatory and the National Maritime museum were there. Were they going to have some sort of nighttime tea trip on the Cutty Sark?

Ella stopped daydreaming about the possibilities of her second date with Fergus and jumped into the shower. She washed her hair, exfoliated, and shaved her legs. Although she knew she wouldn't have her legs on show tonight and definitely didn't want to sleep with Fergus so quickly, she did it for peace of mind, so she would feel sexy. She hopped out of the shower and once dry, applied some cocoa butter to her legs and put on her make up. She switched the radio channel from Classical to Radio 1 which was more upbeat and appropriately trashy to get ready for a date. She opened her wardrobe and chose a deep orange polo neck dress that was figure hugging. She searched for some tights at the bottom of her cupboard and hopped about trying to put them on quickly under the dress. She gave her hair a once over with a brush, smoothing the static that popped up when she put on the tight polo neck and chucked the brush back on her bed. She grabbed a long black coat and a pair of black-heeled boots and headed for the door.

*

Fergus was waiting for Ella outside Greenwich station wrapped up in a sheepskin jacket and a maroon wooly scarf. She was seventeen minutes late.

"I am *so so* sorry Fergus! I completely lost track of time when I was painting."

"That's okay. Hello." They kissed on the cheek.

"Hello," she said with a smile.

"You look stunning," he said.

"Thank you," Ella said shyly sinking her head a little further into her polo neck.

"My pleasure. I bought us some mulled wine. I could smell it around the corner and could do with the warmth! I hope you like it?" He passed her the polystyrene cup and Ella raised her glass for a toast.

"Mmm it smells delicious, thank you. I'd love to know how to make mulled wine." Fergus took Ella's mulled-wine-free arm and started walking out on to the road. "So am I allowed to know where we are going yet?"

"Not quite. It's only a short walk away so you'll find out soon Ella."

Ella loved the way he said her name. The l's rolled off his honeyed tongue and somehow made her name sound longer than it was.

"Okay then Mr. Mysterious. If you're going to play a game, then I'm allowed to too."

"That sounds fair," he said cautiously. "What do you have in mind?"

"Well, I was thinking on the tube that we really don't know that much about each other, yet. And since this is the third time I've seen you in what …" Ella counted the days on her free fingers, "four days, then I think I should know how old you are at least! *So*, I have ten questions I want you to answer."

"Gosh! Have we not been through those preliminary questions? Age, birth place, *gender*?"

"No we have not," Ella said as she rolled her eyes at his last suggestion.

"Okay, fire away!" he said while dodging a cluster of people on the pavement. Ella caught a glimpse of sheet music, a bucket and awful hats; carolers, they *must* be carolers she thought before returning her thoughts to the barrage of questions she was about to fire at Fergus.

"Right, first things first. Number one; how old are you?"

"Thirty four." *Perfect*.

"Number two; where are your family from?"

"Hampshire." *Lovely*. "But from Scotland originally". *That's where the red hair in his beard comes from.*

"Number three; what is your favourite band?"

"Oh really? Are you going to ask me that? Guess …" he said teasingly.

"No, you are not doing the questioning. Answer me please," Ella said in mock anger.

"The Rolling Stones," he said chuckling. *Not bad.*

"Number four; which country have you enjoyed traveling most?"

"Hmm. I'd say Spain, Barcelona in particular." *Barcelona, hmm. Been there so many times with Robbie …*

Ella had spent a lot of time in Spain with Robbie, Spanish being one of the many languages he spoke, and she couldn't help but remember their escapades around the city. She took the last sip of mulled wine and then put both of their cups in the bin that they passed on the left hand side of the pavement.

Ella tore her thoughts away from Robbie and thought about her next question.

"Number five; what book are you reading at the moment?"

"Ernest Hemingway's *For Whom the Bell Tolls*." *One of my favourites.*

Ella nodded her head approvingly.

"Number six; who are you closest to?"

"My sister." *Sweet*.

"Number seven; who's your role model?"

"My father." *Even sweeter.*

"Number eight; what is your favourite cuisine?" Ella asked while playing with his hand.

"Middle eastern." *He couldn't have answered better.*

"Hmm okay." She thought of another question to ask while taking his left hand in hers. But suddenly she felt something cold on Fergus' hand. She looked down and saw there was a gold band on his wedding finger. Her heart stopped. *Is he married?*

Fergus looked at her, urging her next question.

"Err, number nine; what is your idea of a perfect weekend?" she mustered, trying to process this potentially earth-shattering piece of information.

"Oh, doing the crossword over a lazy breakfast, reading, walking along the river. Old man stuff." She hardly heard his reply and was looking at the floor now.

Have the last few days been a total lie? How have I not noticed the ring before?

"So I count nine questions Ella," he stated confidently, unaware of her brewing anxiety. "You've got to make it a good one!"

Ella stopped walking and looked up at him.

"Um, I don't want to dampen the mood but, but I've just noticed you're wearing a wedding ring … are you married?"

Although she tried to hide it, the pain in her face and voice was clear.

"Wow," Fergus chuckled. "That's some tenth question," he said looking at the gold ring. "I forgot to take it off before I came back."

A wave of nausea washed over Ella and her eyes widened. "You're married and you've been dating me?" she asked angrily.

"No, no Ella. You misunderstand me. I forgot to take it off before I came back from abroad," he said casually. "When I go to photograph a war zone, or if I'm doing a travel piece, I wear a wedding band."

Ella stood in confused silence.

"There's no way of saying this without sounding like an absolute idiot but, well, I get a lot of attention out there. Ex-pats, journos, writers … they all like a drink or two and because it's a lonely life and a small world, when someone new comes into town they always get hit on."

It was a mad explanation but for some reason Ella trusted Fergus. She didn't doubt for one second that he was telling the truth and knew in her heart that he didn't have a secret wife stored away somewhere. The feel of the cold ring against her hand had just shocked her and made her realise how much she liked him.

"What, so you wear the ring to ward off beautiful predatory women?" she asked mockingly.

Fergus laughed again. "Exactly. I know it sounds ridiculous but out there it means I get some privacy. I don't like being hunted …"

He grinned as Ella raised her eyebrows at him.

"What can I say Ella, women are drawn to me," he said as he shrugged his shoulders playfully.

"Oh are they Fergus?" she asked flirtatiously.

"Some men can't help it."

"Well for some reason I don't b—" Before Ella could deliver her witty repartie, Fergus had grabbed her around the waist and was kissing her passionately on the lips.

"Sorry," he said, drawing apart from her. "Come on, let me show you what we're doing tonight."

Chapter Six

"He took you to the planetarium?!" Libby exclaimed, so loudly that people in the restaurant turned their heads.

"Yes, it was absolutely incredible," Ella said as she took a sip of Sauvignon Blanc. "He booked us a night tour. I didn't know you could even do that. We had the place to ourselves and an astronomer explained how to use the telescopes and ran us through so many beautiful satellite photographs from mission probes! It was breathtaking." She spoke so fast her excitement was obvious.

"God he is such a smooth operator!"

"Ha ha. He is. A gentleman too."

"So you've had two dates since you met at mine?"

"Uh huh."

"That's crazy. He must really like you – and I can tell you like him because you're about to deny it!" she said while preparing another mouthful of quinoa, avocado and pancetta salad. "And you're pushing your food around your plate like you have no appetite and that, Ella, is not like you."

"Oh okay Sherlock. I like him. I really like him," she confessed guilty. "I mean the last two days have been sensational, and the planetarium! Wow. I had mentioned something about liking astronomy at your party when we all went into the games room."

"When you came back from your patio kiss?" she teased.

"Yeeess," Ella said in response. "I had told him about an article I had just read in the *New Scientist* about signs of life on other planets and that's why he knew I'd like the planetarium." Ella ate a mouthful of pasta and then continued to talk about Fergus.

"He's not really like anybody I've met before. He's nothing like Robbie."

Libby dropped her forkful of avocado. Ella hadn't mentioned Robbie's name since January. She was at a loss as to what to say. "No, he's really not," she said finally. "You know that's the first time you've said his name to me since January the 2nd when you vowed never to think or speak of him again."

"I know. I just wasn't ready before. I was so hurt. It was too painful to talk about him or even acknowledge his existence. But that was ages ago now and I've moved on."

"Well that's great Ella. I never wanted to push you to talk about him when you clearly didn't want to. But I'm glad you feel like he's in the past now." Libby smiled and waved to the waiter to get his attention. She wasn't convinced that Ella was completely over Robbie or the break-up, but she didn't blame her. After all, they had been together for six years and been through so much together. They had bought a house together, dealt with the loss of both of Ella's parents at the same time, and then he had just left her, not because he had stopped loving her but because he had wanted different things from life.

But what did it matter if she still held a flame for him? Robbie was half way across the world and Ella wasn't in any danger of seeing him again anytime soon. Libby was glad Fergus had come into Ella's life with these swooping romantic gestures and adventurous dates just in time for Christmas.

"So where is he taking you tonight?" Libby asked, changing the subject.

"Well I thought *I'd* be the one to choose tonight's dates after he's planned such lovely evenings."

"And where are you taking him?" Libby said as she handed over her debit card to the waiter with the card machine.

"Let me give you some cash Libs," Ella said as she reached into her black leather bag.

"No no, it's my treat – a well done for your exhibition. I insist."

"Oh thank you! The exhibition is so close now, I'm getting nervous," she said.

"No work talk please. I have had *the* worst week dressing the stars. Tell me where you're taking him!?"

"Oh okay," she said chuckling. "I'm taking him to Shoreditch House. He said he's never been before and whilst its no planetarium, I am a member and it'll be fun. Plus I have managed to book out the private bowling lanes! I was so lucky no one else had already."

"So it will be just you two and a barman?" Libby asked.

"And sexy bowling shoes."

*

Ella was sitting on the floor amongst her paintings when Fergus rang.

"Hello?" she said.

"Good morning. I just thought I'd continue this week's tradition and ask you on another date." Ella couldn't help but let the smile on her face spread from ear to ear.

"You haven't had enough of me yet? Even after you saw what an atrocious bowler I am?"

"I might have had enough of your bowling but I haven't had enough of you." It was a cheesy reply, but with his rough smoky voice, Fergus sounded sexy and somehow he pulled it off.

"Well what do you propose for our fourth date?"

"How about you come to mine for dinner?"

"Dinner? An ordinary date? Fergus you ought to be ashamed!" she teased him. "Is dinner adventurous enough for you?" As she heard him laugh at the other end of the phone there was a tinny sounding knock at her front door. "Oh one minute, I think Mark's here to help me transport the paintings to the gallery. I'm going to have to go Fergus, but let me know what time you'd like me to come over and send me your address."

"Okay will do. Good luck with all the wrapping."

"Thanks, see you later! I'm looking forward to it."

"As am I."

Ella let Mark in and put the kettle on to make him a cup of tea. Mark worked for Triangle Gallery transporting paintings to and from venues. Today, he had offered to help Ella move all of her paintings to the Beat Gallery. They discussed how the paintings were going to fit in his van and how many trips it would take while they sipped down the warm brew. They spent the whole morning wrapping all of Ella's paintings carefully in foam and bubble wrap and the afternoon scuttling between Ella's studio and the Beat Gallery, which was only thirty minutes down the road. The weather had taken another colder turn and the roads were beginning to ice over a bit, causing their journeys to take a little longer.

On the final return trip back to Ella's studio, light snowflakes began to fall. Ella looked out at the delicate flakes mesmerized and thought about the evening ahead of her. Tonight she was going to Fergus' house and she had a feeling she might be staying the night. Although they had only known each other for less than a week, after four dates Ella felt ready to take that step with him.

The car pulled up outside her studio and Mark's voice startled her out of her daydream.

"Good luck with tha exbition Ellah," he said in his cockney accent that was so strong that Ella thought it could not be a hundred percent genuine. "Let me know 'ow it goes afterwards."

"I will Mark. Thank you for all your help today. You've been such a star!"

"No worries luv. Now be careful wit tha ice."

Ella closed the van door behind her and walked to her front door. The snow that had fallen was so light it wasn't settling. Ella wished that just once the snow in London wouldn't melt as soon as it touched the dirty city streets.

She stepped into her studio and went straight to the bathroom to prune, prep and groom herself for the approaching date.

*

Ella arrived at Fergus' flat in Islington at seven thirty with a bottle of Rioja in hand. He greeted her at the door with a kiss and ushered her in, taking her blue mohair coat and hanging it up on his coat rack. Underneath her coat, she was wearing a long-sleeved black silk dress that had a dipped neckline, emphasizing her cleavage. Her hair was swept off her face into a short ponytail exposing her neck. This was the first time Fergus had seen Ella dressed in something more revealing than winter polo necks and coats. His expression reflected her outfit's success and she blushed at the way he looked at her. He took her in his arms, placed his arm around the small of her back and kissed her on the lips.

"Are you hungry?" he asked.

"Yes I am. Can I help with anything?"

"Well actually yes, you can help with a lot." He had a suspicious grin on his face.

"Okay," she said nervously. "Show me to the kitchen."

They walked through a large Victorian living room with a beautiful open fireplace. The walls were adorned with black and white prints from floor to ceiling and two comfortable looking grey sofas were positioned in an L shape around the fireplace. On the left of the fireplace was a medium-sized Christmas tree covered in red and gold glittering baubles. Ella stopped to admire the wooden carvings of angels and reindeer, which hung delicately on the smaller branches. On the top of the tree was a striking dove with a long glistening tail, perching where the star normally went.

"Come on," Fergus said, prompting Ella to follow him into the kitchen.

To her surprise, there was a short, dark-haired Mediterranean man in the kitchen, standing over the cooker.

"Ella, this is Luigi. He is going to be our teacher tonight. We'll be cooking some authentic Italian food."

"Oh wow. It's lovely to meet you Luigi," Ella said as she shook the chef's hand. "Fergus this is an amazing idea."

"Not bad for a 'normal' dinner date eh?" he asked mischievously, walking around the kitchen island to organise the pile of ingredients which stood on a thick wooden chopping board.

"Not bad at all," Ella replied.

"Ima gonna teach you 'ow to make Italian winterr dishes. *Arancini*, deep fried balls ofa risotto, *Sicilian fish soup* and *Polpette di pollo*, which is chicken ameataballs in rich tomato sawce."

Ella was besides herself. "Incredible."

"He's also given me a recipe for mulled wine, which we could make after. You mentioned you'd love to know how to make it when we went to the planetarium."

"Oh Fergus." Ella was lost for words. This man was so thoughtful and clearly listened to everything that came out of her mouth. "I'm totally bowled over by your kindness. You've put so much thought into all our dates it's, it's …" Ella was truly stunned for words.

Fergus walked around the island and gave her a kiss on the lips.

"It's all been so fun to organise for you."

"Thank you," she said quietly. She could feel that Luigi didn't know where to look, while the couple had their moment of tenderness. He turned back to the cooker and stirred one of his pots.

Ella cleared her throat.

"Is mulled wine an Italian dish?" she proposed to Fergus. "I though it was British?"

"Ah it's a British tradition to drink it at Christmas, but wine was first recorded as spiced and heated in Rome in the 2nd century."

"Ah yes, the Romans. Where would we be without them? I have no doubt Luigi has a smashing recipe for it."

Fergus and Ella spent the evening laughing, tasting and questioning Luigi about Italian cuisine as they attempted each dish.

Ella was particularly good at making the arancini, skillfully forming the round balls of pistachio, cheese, tomato and oregano in a layer of risotto that was cooked in white wine and Parmesan. Luigi demonstrated how to roll each circle in flour and breadcrumbs carefully so that no rice was peeking through. They set the balls aside to be fried later while they made haste on the soup.

Luigi set Fergus to work on the chopping, while he showed Ella how to fillet the fresh fish. The broth was made with fennel, onions, chilli, and garlic and once this concoction had been simmering for some time and the onions were soft, they added passata and butternut squash. The dish came to life when the wonderful colours of the salmon, halibut, langoustine and parsley were all thrown in. As it bubbled away, the flavours doubling, Luigi fried the arancini. They ate the risotto balls that oozed with melted Parmesan and oregano as a starter and gently stirred the soup while discussing the next dish.

They blitzed the bread, olives, capers, garlic and Parmesan in the blender and then added the chunks of chicken and an egg to bind the mixture together. Once rolled into small balls, they placed them in the oven to cook.

As they watched the meatballs brown, they sat down at the table, to feast on the soup that was light and tangy.

"This soup is absolutely delicious Luigi!" cried Ella.

"It's wonderful!" said Fergus.

"Justa wait 'til you try the meataballs! Save some room ah?" Luigi set to work on the tomato sugo while Ella and Fergus enjoyed their soup and talked about Christmas traditions.

"Stockings at the end of the bed or hanging on the fireplace?" Fergus asked.

"Oh always at the fire place. We used to scramble down stairs at hourly intervals throughout the night to see if they had been filled!"

"Gosh I remember that excitement as a child. You said 'we', do you have siblings?"

"Yes I have one older brother, called Jimi."

"Don't tell me he's named after another singer? Jimi Hendrix?" Fergus asked with a wry smile.

Ella chuckled. "Not that I know of. He was christened James, like my father."

"Ah I see. So how do you spend your Christmas with your family? Do you go back to your parents house still?" he asked, tilting his bowl towards him to scoop out the last of the soup. Ella knew as soon as he asked that question that she would have to tell him that her parents had passed away. It was a conversation she dreaded having, not least because no one ever knew how to react to it but because it was just as painful to say it out loud now, as it was when it happened.

"I'm actually spending it with the Crosleys. My parents died in a car crash five years ago. Jimi's away on business so I'm spending it with Libby."

"Oh Ella, I'm so sorry. I didn't know that your parents had passed away."

"It's okay. Well obviously it's not okay, it's hard. But, well you learn to live with it," she said, leaning back on her chair, becoming aware again of Luigi's clattering of pans. "I try to focus on my memories of my mother and father and not of the pain of the past five years. I talk about them but I don't really talk about *it* to anyone, anymore."

Fergus understood that *it* must be a reference to the car crash and could see that Ella did not want to divulge any more on the matter. She looked fidgety, moving around restlessly in her chair. He squeezed her hand and tried to change the subject for her sake.

"So where is your brother for business then? What does he do?"

"He is a doctor and he has a medical convention in Prague," she said, visibly relaxing. "He sent me some photos the other day. It looks so beautiful at this time of year."

"Oh, I bet it must be with all the Christmas markets and the striking buildings topped with snow dusted spirals," he replied.

"Mmm," she nodded while taking a sip of her wine. "I'm so jealous they'll have snow."

"Me too. Wouldn't it be lovely if the snow falling now settled and we had a White Christmas?"

"Oh I would adore it, just so long as it wasn't so thick I couldn't drive out to the Crosley's in Kent."

Luigi interrupted them with the arresting smell of bubbling tomato, crisped chicken and freshly chopped parsley.

"'Ere you go. Youra last dish!" He placed the plate in the middle of the table, between the silvery candles that were burning brightly.

"Oh thank you so much!" Ella cried in excitement.

"My pleasure! Now I musta leave you to enjoy all ayour harda worka!"

Fergus and Ella got up to thank Luigi for such a pleasant evening and Fergus showed him to the door. When he came back to the table, Ella had poured them some more wine and raised her glass for a toast.

"Here's to a magical week!"

"And, to a White Christmas!" he replied hopefully as they chinked glasses.

After they recovered from their feast, they set to work on the mulled wine. Fergus put on some music while Ella stirred the pot of stewing spices. They were a little tipsy as they maneuvered around the kitchen clearing up the mess they had created. They hummed along and moved lightly to the sweet sounds of Nat King Cole's voice as he smoothly sung 'The First Noël'. Ella tasted the mulled wine and deemed it ready. It was scrumptious, with the perfect balance of orange, cinnamon and cloves. She offered a spoonful to Fergus to try over the cooker. He took a sip and beamed.

"It's divine," he whispered as he stared into her eyes.

He turned off the hob, put his arms around Ella's tiny waist and kissed her passionately as the King sang something about snow and mistletoe.

His hands moved over her hips, tickling her slightly through the silk material of her dress that clung to her skin. She ran her hands through his hair and they started walking backwards away from the cooker. They bumped into the island as they kissed with their eyes closed and stumbled through to the living room. Fergus took Ella's hand and led her to bedroom.

Chapter Seven

Ella woke up with Fergus' muscular arms wrapped around her body. She opened her eyes and saw his sleepy face staring back at her. The dark and cozy room smelt of pine and the fading scent of Fergus' musty cologne.

"Good morning you," he whispered.

"Morning," she croaked, her throat dry from last night's wine.

"It's your big day today," he said, brushing a strand of her hair from off her face. "I'm excited to finally see some of your paintings."

"Oh yes. I'm a little bit nervous," she admitted. "I hope enough people come." Ella yawned and stretched across the bed.

"Hey, where are you going?" he said, playfully pulling her back towards him. "It's going to be a *huge* success. Now, would you like some breakfast?"

"I'd love some coffee please." They kissed lightly on the lips and Fergus moved to open the curtains while Ella straightened out the duvet on her side of the bed.

Light flooded the room and they were temporarily blinded by the brightness. All they saw was white.

"Snow!" Fergus exclaimed.

It took Ella a few seconds to adjust and realize that the white before her wasn't just the daylight appearing stronger because of the prior darkness of the room, it was snow laid thickly as far as the eyes could see.

"Ah! Snow! Ohh it's so beautiful!" she said happily. She observed the street in all its snowy glory; the Victorian town houses doused in a sprinkling of snow, the pavement covered in a layer a few inches deep and the children on their school run with snowballs in hand.

Fergus held Ella from behind as they looked joyfully over the snowy scene in front of them.

"Our wish might have worked Ell."

"It seems it has. I hope it stays until Christmas Day. Oh, but I hope everybody can still make it to the gallery tonight."

"I'm sure they will."

Ella got dressed while Fergus made a pot of coffee. When she came into the kitchen wearing her silky black dress from the night before, Fergus couldn't help but smile.

"Hello sexy," he said, looking up from the coffee he was pouring into two small orange espresso cups.

"Hi," Ella replied with a smirk. The rich aroma of freshly ground Columbian coffee woke Ella up a little but it wasn't strong enough to mask the lingering spices and stale acidic smell of the mulled wine.

"I can still smell the mulled wine," she said.

"Mmm. Pungent! It's a shame we didn't drink any. Well not that much of a shame …"

Ella blushed a little.

"Want some?" he joked.

"I musn't. I'm on a wine-free breakfast diet at the moment," she teased in reply. "But I must leave after this." She gestured to the coffee. "I have a lot to sort at the gallery before this evening."

"Of course." They sipped their coffee in the living room while Ella looked at Fergus' photographs. The wall behind his sofa was lined with black and white prints she hadn't had the opportunity to look at the night before. Most of his photos were filled with dust, dirt, destruction and despair. They were beautiful in their simplicity but harrowing at the same time. Ella noticed that his photos were taken from unique angles but they weren't artificial in any way. He used a film camera and as such didn't edit his photographs in an attempt to turn them into something they were not. No photoshop, no lies.

Fergus watched Ella look at his walled collection and wondered what she thought of them. She had observed them in silence for a few minutes, which was beginning to unsettle him.

"These are magnificent Fergus. You are *so so* talented. I love this one especially."

She pointed to a portrait of an old Iraqi man. He was slouching asleep on a chair at his post. His right hand was clasping the body of a large machine gun against his chest and his other arm had gone limp in his sleepy state. It had fallen away from his body sloping down to the dusty ground and his palm was facing upwards. Next to his open hand was a small bird pecking at the barren earth. It almost looked like the man was feeding this little creature while he was asleep.

"I'm glad you like them," Fergus said.

"I do. I think they are all phenomenal. I'd love to see more of them when I have more time."

"Any time," he said as they sipped the last of their coffee. Fergus returned the mugs to the kitchen while Ella fetched her coat from the hangers by the front door.

"Good luck with all the preparations today. I'll see you later." Fergus leant in to kiss Ella and held her fast in his arms. Ella did not want this kiss to end, she wanted to relive last night and crawl back into bed with him but she knew today was not the day. She had to get back to her apartment to change and head straight to the gallery.

She finally tore herself from his arms and said goodbye. She walked down the stairs leading to the ground floor and opened the main building door to the snow-covered street. She skipped down the steps to the pavement and floated to Highbury and

Islington tube station with an absurdly wide grin on face and a spring in her step.

*

Ella arrived at the Beat Gallery at eleven o'clock. She walked through the spacious venue that had once been an old Victorian railway station. It was the perfect space for a contemporary art exhibition; it's enormous arched ceilings provided enough space for the larger paintings in her collection. Her pieces were leant against the walls where Ella presumed they were to be hung. Ella saw the gallery staff, Sophie, Guy and Daisy discussing something, pointing and gesturing passionately towards different corners of the gallery.

"Ella, hi!" a tanned voluptuous figure called from the opposite end of the gallery. This was Celia, the gallery manager. She was holding an armful of small brown parcels that she put on the table closest to her. She glided over to Ella.

"Hello Celia! How are we all?" Ella asked, waving at the others in the gallery.

"Fantastic! The others were just discussing where each painting should go. We thought we'd wait for you to arrive before we hung any." Celia smiled, flashing a perfect set of white teeth. Her uniform teeth shone brightly against her molasses-coloured skin and her amethyst eyes burned vibrantly.

"Great. Thank you Celia. You've all done a great job. The gallery looks magnificent and so Christmassy!"

The gallery staff had found some unique fairy lights that could be hung vertically from the ceiling. They bought and installed three hundred of these individual lights that now dangled down to just above everyone's heads. The function was threefold; to illuminate the paintings, to make the gallery look festive and to fill up some of the space in the venue. They looked marvelous even in the daylight and Ella could tell that when it was dark outside and the main gallery lights were switched off, the place was going to look magical with these glowing orbs.

"So do you like the positions of the paintings? Can we put them up?" Celia asked. Ella walked over to Daisy, Guy and Sophie who were huddling around 'Toasted Sunset'. The brush strokes of burnt orange were bursting into life, flaming wildly in the well-lit gallery.

Ella walked through the gallery several times; she moved from the front door, down the winding corridor-shaped room and back again. The room was tall and narrow with brilliant white walls and one sea-blue feature wall. Makeshift walls had been erected in the middle of the room where more of her paintings were to be shown. The structure created two channels so guests would have to walk through one corridor and back up the other. Alternatively, they could snake through the middle paintings, weaving in and out of the small temporary walls. This layout had been cleverly designed. It meant that most paintings could be seen from all angles of the room so viewers could either focus on the painting in front of them or turn to see the whole collection at once.

Seeing the paintings in their places was making Ella excited. Her very first exhibition! She had waited so long for this moment. She had worked so hard for the last few years behind the scenes at the Triangle gallery and now it was all coming to fruition. If it went well she might be able to work fewer days in the gallery and devote more time to being an artist in her own right. Taking the leap to professional artist was risky. It wasn't a stable job and it wouldn't be lucrative unless she was very lucky and in the right place at the right time. She felt tremendous appreciation for her colleagues at the Triangle Gallery. They had helped her to secure this exhibition as they had praised her artwork to the Beat Gallery's owner and told him to check out her art.

Luckily, the owner took to Ella's paintings and now she was standing in London's coolest, newest, most talked about gallery with her paintings on the wall!

Ella was staring at the ceiling that was ablaze with fairy lights. She had her hand over her mouth trying to contain the sheer joy she was feeling. She was awestruck. Things were starting to go her way again. Her career, her love life …

"Erm, Ella? What do you think to the arrangement then? Do you not like it?" Daisy inquired nervously.

"Oh no, I love it!" Ella gasped, returning to reality. "Sorry I was just … I was just thinking about this evening."

"So are you happy with how it is? Shall we start fixing them?" Guy asked gruffly. The red rings around his eyes warned Ella that he was not in a good mood. He looked tired and in dire need of a coffee. Had he been out last night or was he being over-worked by the gallery? Ella hoped it wasn't because of her exhibition. Things were already awkward enough between them; ever since Guy had asked her on a date that had led nowhere, they felt uncomfortable in each other's presence. After Ella had broken up with Robbie, Guy asked her out repeatedly until she finally said yes. Ella knew she only saw Guy as a friend and that going on a date wouldn't change that, but she couldn't bring herself to refuse him a fourth time and she had thought it might be a good distraction from her heartbreak. They had had a lovely time at a concert on Primrose Hill, but Ella had made it clear at the end of the evening that she didn't see Guy in a romantic way.

"Yes, I am happy. They all look wonderful," she replied in as cheery voice as she could manage. "Thank you Guy," she added tenderly.

"Great, come with me Ella." Celia beckoned her to come into the gallery office and she followed without pause.

They stood in the doorway of the office, talking business. Celia was sifting through guest lists and reminding Ella who were the most important guests of the evening. As she spoke, Ella was overlooking the painting hanging. While Celia was twiddling with her hair and chatting on about *saddling up to the right contacts*, Ella noticed that something wasn't quite right. She had just seen one of her paintings from a new angle.

"Sorry guys," she called out to the team. "I've just noticed we have a bit of a colour block over there. The background of that feature wall is very blue and just in front of it is 'Midnight Water'. I think it looks a bit lost there – it's swamped by its surroundings."

The others took a step back towards the office where Ella and Celia were standing and squinted at the painting.

"You're right!" said the high-pitched Sophie. "All those lovely blues are swamped by the blue feature wall."

"Would you mind swapping that one with 'Dawn II' please? I think the pinks in that will really stand out against the blue and then we can put 'Midnight Water' where 'Dawn II' was on the white wall. They are roughly the same size so it should fit," Ella replied thoughtfully.

"Of course," Daisy remarked as the other two followed her to swap the paintings. Ella thought she could hear Guy mumble something under his breath but she didn't catch it, whatever it was.

*

It took several hours to hang all of the paintings and clean up the gallery. The gallery staff tested the lighting and hung a few more Christmas decorations. Sophie tied bunches of mistletoe amongst the fairy lights hung from the ceiling. Exhausted, the team slumped on the sofas in the office and looked proudly on what they had created. Through the door of the office, they could see the whole room was glowing. The fairy lights bounced off the paintings and added a wonderful festive atmosphere.

"I've just got off the phone with Hugh, he's going to bring some takeaway to the office so we can eat before the opening," Celia said.

"Great. I'm starving," Guy replied, perking up a bit.

Ella excused herself and went to the bathroom to change and touch up her make-up. She put on an asymmetrical, Japanese-style, black wrap-around dress. It was made of rough satin and had a silvery shine in some lights.

She took out her YSL mascara but she couldn't apply it. Her hands were shaking. She was nervous. Would enough people show up? Were they going to like her paintings? Ella steadied her nerves and breathed slowly in and out. She waited until she was slightly calmer before she applied some NARS smoky eye shadow. She curled her eyelashes, coated them lightly in mascara and put on a red-orange MAC lipstick called *Lady Danger*. It complimented her skin tone and brought out the brown in her eyes. Once she had finished applying her make-up she rejoined the others in the office to be greeted by cries of "Wow", "You look stunning!" and in Guy's case, stunned silence with his lower jaw hanging so far open, Daisy actually had to shut it. Clearly, he was still in to her. Ella smiled embarrassingly and thanked everyone.

She felt her nerves jittering again, a lump in her stomach rising up, trying to escape up through her throat. Feeling light-headed, she placed a hand on the back of the sofa to steady herself.

"What's wrong Ella?" Daisy asked with concern.

"Oh, I'm just nervous. Being centre of attention, people showing up etc. I'll be fine in a minute."

"Oh don't worry about numbers! On the facebook event alone it says over two hundred people are coming and there are lots of people from the art world that we invited that aren't on facebook. So they'll be more than two hundred people here tonight! Don't worry!" Daisy reassured her.

"Daisy's right. Look at the page," Sophie said, while getting up the event page on her phone.

"*Ella Moore Exhibition at the Beat*: *Opening Night*. 243 attending, 67 maybe, 59 invited. *See*!" Sophie squeaked.

A look of relief flooded Ella's face. She was starting to feel more confident about the opening now and the sense of excitement she felt earlier was coming back to her. Just as Ella sighed and sat back in the sofa, Hugh bounced through the gallery front door. He strode through the main room, his eyes feasting on the room as his portly stomach wobbled and his grey ponytail swung from side to side. Hugh was the owner of the Beat Gallery who had come across her paintings at the Triangle. Once he saw them, he set about organizing her first exhibition immediately.

"Right, who's hungry for Chinese?" he bellowed as he lifted the bags of steaming food up in the air. "This place looks great by the way! You've transformed it in the last few hours!"

The whole team settled in to their takeaway and Ella was careful not to drop any food on her dress or smudge her lipstick. When they finished eating, it was almost seven o'clock so Daisy, Guy and Sophie double-checked all the paintings were straight, arranged the glasses for drinks and briefed the waiters who had just arrived. Celia, as manager and Hugh, as owner, stayed with Ella in the office and toasted to the hopeful success of the exhibition. After being given the all-clear from the staff, Celia asked if Ella was ready to open the doors. It was seven thirty and people were already congregating outside.

"Absolutely. Open the doors," Ella replied cheerily. She topped up her glass of champagne and walked into the gallery to greet people. She felt better now. All of her anxieties had disappeared and were replaced with immense joy.

Steadily the room started to fill with a mixture of friends, family and artists. Her colleagues from the Triangle gallery were the first to arrive, ever eager to support one of their own. Next came her friends; Libby, Charlie, Lara, Harry, Toby, Emily and even Marcus and Jessica were there. Then Mr and Mrs Crosley arrived with some of their older friends who she hoped might be interested in buying some of her pictures. Ella was rushed off her feet. She had to greet all the guests and was being pulled to and fro by Hugh and Celia who were eager to introduce her to as many influential people as possible.

Before she knew it, it was nine thirty already and Ella had to stop to catch her breath. She had spent a solid two hours recycling the same spiel. She stole away to the bathroom, and when she returned, she found Fergus had arrived. He was wearing an aviator jacket lined with thick sheepskin over a plain black t-shirt, a pair of black jeans and tan desert boots. He looked gorgeous and Ella blushed thinking about last night. He walked straight up to her and kissed her on the cheek.

"Ella it looks beautiful. You are so bloody talented!" he shouted in excitement.

"Thank you. Do you really like them?" Ella asked, speaking louder now to be heard over the growing chatter in the room.

"Yes! Incredible!" he said. "I've just done a lap and seen all of them. I can't wait to learn more about them from *you*, the *artist*."

She smiled and squeezed his hand, drawing closer to him. They stood facing one of her paintings and she explained what it was inspired by, where she had painted it and what it meant to her. He couldn't keep his eyes off her as they stood holding hands, her face glowing with happiness and the lights hanging above her.

"I'm so glad you're here," she said to him. "It's been so busy. I've barely seen Libby and the gang. I haven't even been able to get a drink. Every time a waiter comes near me all his or her glasses are pinched by someone else before me!"

"Well, can I fix that for you. What would you like to drink, champagne?"

"Oh yes please," she replied thankfully.

Ella turned back to face the painting she and Fergus had been looking at. It was her favourite one and she pondered it silently.

She had been looking at it for a few moments when she heard a gasp from the other end of the room. Through the gaps in the crowd, Ella could see Libby looking bewildered, scarred even. She wondered what was happening, but someone walked in front of her and blocked her view. She stood by the painting and looked to the bar area for Fergus; when he returned they would check everything was okay with her friends. She spotted him talking to the waiter who was manning the temporary bar. It looked like they were discussing her paintings, as they were both gesturing energetically to different corners of the room. Ella forgot about Libby's pained expression. She felt a small pang of pride as she watched Fergus and the young woman praise her paintings. She turned happily to look at her favourite painting once again, when she felt a hand on her hip and heard a familiar voice.

"Hi Ella," a well-spoken voice whispered. Ella's whole body tensed.

She turned around slowly to meet a pair of hazelnut eyes. Robbie's eyes.

Chapter Eight

Ella froze. She was gripped by surprise as their eyes locked. Shock started seeping in her body as the blood started draining from her face. Ella opened her mouth to speak but nothing came out; she looked like a fish out of water gasping for air. Robbie was smiling nervously and took a step towards her.

Was Robbie really standing there in front of her? Was it really *him*?

Ella had imagined him showing up in front of her just like this countless times. She had searched for his face in every crowd, secretly hoped that he was going to return to London and win her back again. Every face that she had passed in the street bore some sort of resemblance to him. She saw suited Robbies, homeless Robbies, busking Robbies, janitor Robbies, builder Robbies … she had seen every different version of Robbie as she wondered through London like a zombie overwhelmed with heartbreak. For so long any and every stranger had taken on his characteristics until day-by-day she started to see his face less and less and eventually she saw it no more.

Now, the one time in the last year she didn't want to see him, the one place she didn't want him to be, she saw him.

Robbie broke the tense silence first and put his hand on her arm.

"I wanted to see you Ella. I'm so sorry, so sorry about everything. We need to talk." He raised his hand to stroke her cheek and she wanted to slap it away but she was paralysed by his presence, dumbfounded by the face she knew so well. She just stared at him thinking *how has he heard about my exhibition and why is he here?*

Finally, she plucked up the strength to speak.

"What are you doing here?" she said in a quiet but threatening hiss.

"Ella please, I know this isn't the best place but please see me later."

"How dare you come here!" she replied angrily, stepping back away from him. She was no longer pale and lacking energy. She was flustered and her face was a terrifying shade of red, darkening by the second. She had spoken as loudly as she could without startling the people around her but she wanted nothing more than to scream at him.

"Ella, please. I know I have no right to be here or demand anything from you but you can't deny that we need to speak. Oh Ella. You look so gorgeous. So very, very Ella. And the exhibition is amazing. I'm so proud of you."

Fury was bubbling inside of Ella now. He had some nerve coming to her exhibition, telling her how *gorgeous* she looked, how *amazing* her paintings were and how *proud* he was of her. The cheek!

"You're *proud* of me? Do you have *any* idea of what you've put me through?" she said, panting with rage. "I want you to leave *now*." It was a command not a request. Her face almost matched the colour of her lips. *Lady Danger* had arrived.

"Ella, just promise me you'll meet me tomorrow night? There is something I need to tell you — something I need to *ask* you. *S'il vous plaît Ella. Je t'adore*." There was an urgency in Robbie's voice that Ella's heart couldn't ignore. Despite sounding anguished, his voice still soothed her. This was the voice that had consoled her after her parents had died, the voice that had told her he loved her in five different languages. Suddenly all the sweet nothings Robbie had whispered into her ears over the years came flooding back to her. She tried desperately to hold back her tears. She didn't understand why he was here and why she was so attracted to him still.

His suit fit his muscular frame so well. His hair had grown longer and was now slicked back a little, curling at the sides of his ears. It suited him and Ella hated that it did. She tried to contain her attraction to him and forced herself to warn him off again.

"I will see you *only* if you leave *right now*," Ella said through gritted teeth. She was trying to hold back her emotion, like a frenzied racehorse being held behind its gate before a race. She didn't want to cause a scene in the middle of her opening night and she didn't want to know what would happen when the gun went off and the horse was released from its starting gate. She couldn't let anybody see her breakdown, not here.

"Okay, okay," Robbie said gently. His face was more tanned than usual and his skin looked so smooth that she wanted to touch it. She also wanted to hit it.

"The paintings really are amazing," he continued, not leaving. "I've bought all the ones you painted while we were together." Suddenly, outrage filled Ella from top to toe. Her eyes narrowed on him menacingly. She didn't want him to own *anything* of hers, least of all her paintings! Was he deliberately trying to taunt her? Was he trying to claim part of her after having cast her aside? Her art was her life. Did stealing her heart not satisfy him enough? Did he have to take her art too?

"I cannot believe you would —"

"My favourite is this one," he said as he pointed to 'Midnight Water', the painting hanging on the left of them. "Do you remember where you painted that? We were in the villa in Italy. We were staring out at the sea at midnight and you were painting half naked, wrapped only in the bedspread. You've added something —"

"Go." This was the last time Ella would warn him.

Robbie could see that she truly meant it, that she had not been the least bit impressed at his attempts to resurrect the memories of their past or that he had bought her paintings. That was probably a step too far, he thought. Ella was protective of her art.

Robbie finally backed off. He said "See you tomorrow" and disappeared into the crowd.

Ella could see Libby and Charlie trying to clamber through the room of guests towards her. But on seeing which direction Robbie was going in, Charlie changed his course. It looked like he was about to confront Robbie or escort him out. Somebody stepped in front of Ella to get closer to one of her paintings and in doing so blocked her view of Robbie and Charlie.

While Ella had been facing Robbie, Fergus had been walking back to find her. With their drinks in his hand, he had turned to see a tall handsome man brush Ella's cheek tenderly. Fergus stopped in his tracks as he watched on and saw Ella's gaze turn from shock to fury. He knew he and Ella had only just started dating but seeing another man that close to Ella made him feel sick. He walked slowly through the busy crowd, dodging between people but never taking his eyes off the mysterious man who was talking to the beautiful woman he was infatuated with. As he got closer to them, he caught the man say the word *Italy*. Fergus struggled to hear him above the Christmassy jazz that was tinkering out of the gallery speakers. He tried to move forwards but there was a large woman, who was more than festively plump, blocking his way. She was moving this way and that, mirroring his movements so he couldn't get past her. *Naked.* The second word he heard piqued his interest further and he pushed passed the grotesque woman with more force this time. *Leave.* It was Ella's voice this time and it seemed to have an effect as Fergus saw the sun-kissed man sink away into the hubbub of artists.

Finally, Fergus reached Ella's side and turned to look at her tomato face. He had never imagined someone so gentle could look so mad and he was almost scared to ask her if she was okay.

"Ella?" Fergus asked mildly. "Is everything okay?"

She was breathing fast, her heart heaving in her chest and she was still staring at the man who was making his way back through the crowd. The man she had loved for so long. She turned to Fergus, the beautiful kind Fergus. She relaxed on seeing him. She took one of the glasses of champagne he had brought over and downed it in one.

"Yes. I'm sorry. Thank you for the drink." She tried to force a smile but it was no good. She felt as if someone had dropped an anvil on her head and the pressure of seeing Robbie again was squashing her.

"Who was that?" Fergus asked inquisitively.

"It was an old friend. A ghost you might say." Ella didn't want to talk about Robbie's appearance. She certainly didn't want to explain who he was now to Fergus. She didn't want to drag her past into the new relationship. She had wanted a new slate. Clearly, that had been too much to ask! She didn't need to explain who Robbie was because he wasn't a part of her life anymore. *Was he?*

Ella could see Fergus' confusion and felt she needed to tell him something more.

"He's a friend from my past that I didn't expect to see. If you don't mind, I don't want to talk about it right now. I'd like to focus on my exhibition, my work." As she uttered the words, she remembered bitterly that Robbie had just bought her work.

Fergus could see how upset Ella was and he knew how much this exhibition meant to her, so he tried to distract her.

"Of course. Well, I invited someone, a photographer called Zac Tobin. I'd like you to meet him. Apparently he's already a fan of your art." Ella was nodding to the floor. She wiped a single tear from her eye and looked up at Fergus.

She forced Robbie to the back of her mind and smiled bravely deciding she must soldier on. Her guests would be gone by eleven o'clock. She just needed to get through the next few hours and she didn't want Fergus to read too much in to her reaction to Robbie, if that was at all possible.

"Lovely," she replied. "I would adore to meet your friend. I can see Libby coming over, let's take her with us." Ella beckoned Libby to follow them, aware that her best friend was bursting to ask about Robbie's appearance and check if she was okay. When she managed to squeeze by a group of people to get to Ella, Libby stood by her side and they communicated solely with their eyes using a language that was reserved only for women. They understood each other perfectly: Libby flashed Ella an *Are you okay? What the fuck was he doing here?* look. Ella widened her eyes and replied with an *I don't fucking know*, *I'm so mad but I need to get through this night*, *let's talk about it later* look. Fergus introduced them both to Zac and they talked about cubism until Hugh came over. He needed to steal Ella away for a minute.

Ella was glad to be out of Fergus' concerned gaze. She spent the rest of the evening talking to artists and repressing her heartache. Everybody seemed to be having a jolly time, everybody except her. As it approached eleven o'clock, the gallery emptied out. Ella waved goodbye to her colleagues from the Triangle gallery and kissed William and Elisabeth Crosley goodbye, thanking them for bringing along so many friends.

There were only a few people left when Hugh came out with a bottle of Dom Pérignon and proposed a toast to Ella.

"You, Miss Moore, have broken the record for most paintings ever sold on the opening night of an exhibition at the Beat Gallery! Guess how many were bought?"

Everybody muttered numbers excitedly and someone suggested, "Seventeen?"

"Noo ... all of them!" Hugh bellowed with joy.

There was a little round of applause as the gallery staff and all her friends congratulated her. She should have been thrilled at this but knowing Robbie had bought so many of them made her feel sick.

"So are we going to go out now and celebrate? Any good bars around here?" Harry asked.

Ella had put on a brave face for hours but she new she couldn't last much longer.

"I would absolutely love to. And I am so grateful for you all coming and supporting me. You've all been incredible and so encouraging and helpful. But I am completely shattered after such a busy week preparing for the exhibition. I'm going to be terribly boring and go home. I think I would collapse in the middle of the dance floor if I came out!" Ella spoke as cheerily as she could.

It seemed that everyone had been convinced by her performance and they all smiled sweetly at her speech. Charlie, Libby and Fergus however were flashing her anxious looks, guessing correctly that the dramatic scene that had unfolded earlier was the real reason she wasn't going out for celebratory drinks. They could tell that she wasn't her normal self.

Ella hugged everybody goodbye, collected her belongings from the office and walked to the front door with Fergus. Libby and Charlie followed close behind them, but left enough distance that they could say goodbye in private.

Ella took Fergus' hand as they entered the cold and snowy night.

"Thank you for coming tonight Fergus. It means a lot that you did. Last night was perfect."

Fergus kissed Ella on the head and wrapped her scarf around her neck. He told her what a fantastic evening he had had and how sensational her art was. Ella noticed that Fergus' mesmerising blue eyes looked a little sad.

"I'll call you tomorrow?" she asked.

"I look forward to it. I hope you're okay Ella."

She smiled, kissed him on the cheek and turned to Libby and Charlie who were waiting for her. Fergus sauntered down the road and looked back at Ella, who was now being sandwiched by two caring friends.

"Right, I'm taking you home. I'm staying with you tonight darling," Libby said. They hugged

Charlie goodbye and stepped into the slushy melting snow that had gathered where the pavement met the road. They flagged down a black cab and left the glow of the gallery behind them.

*

Libby made Ella a cup of hot chocolate topped with nutmeg and brought it over to the bed where she was tucked up. She looked distraught, just like she had done when Robbie had left her last Christmas time.

"I am SO mad at him Ella! I can't even imagine what you must be going through," Libby puffed. "How could he just show up like that after a year of nothing? No contact. No phone call. No explanation. Only a fucking note!"

Ella's eyes were glazed over. Her knees up by her face and she was resting her hot chocolate on top of them. She stared into her mug. She looked childlike and fragile in her muted turmoil.

"I don't understand," she whispered finally. "It's just so unfair. He's so selfish."

Libby took off her shoes and jeans, took a pair of pyjama bottoms from Ella's cupboard and sat down next to her in the bed.

"Incredibly selfish. I wish I had got to him first. I was bloody shocked. We should have stopped him as soon as we saw him. I'm sorry Ell."

"Oh please Libs, don't apologise. It's not your fault," she said as she put the mug to her lips and drank some of the warming chocolate. "He was so determined to talk to me I doubt anything would have stopped him. You know what he's like."

"I thought Charlie was going to punch him right in the middle of the gallery when I saw him follow Robbie off. I'm not sure if he caught up with Robbie but I know he tried. He's so protective of you."

"I know. God, I would have liked to see him punch Robbie," Ella said passionately. She started to cry again. "I just ... why now? What does he want?" she said through sobs. "I was just getting over him and I've just met Fergus and he comes crashing back into my life like a bulldozer."

"Did you get an idea from him of what he was doing here? What he wants? What did he actually say to you? Does he want to be back with you, is that why he was here?"

"I don't know. It's all a bit of a blur to be honest. He said he was sorry. He said he had something to tell me. Something to ask me." Ella finished the rest of her drink.

"Ask you?" Libby questioned.

"Yup." Ella shrugged. Robbie had caused her so much pain over the last year. She had spent too many days curled under her duvet in the dark wishing it were all a nightmare when he first left. Was she back to square one now that he was back?

"Are you going to meet him tomorrow?" Libby asked, taking the empty mug and placing it on the bedside table. Ella fluffed up her pillow and sank into her friend's shoulder. Libby smelt of the orange body lotion she had worn since they were teenagers. The citrus smell comforted her.

"Do you think I should?" Ella asked as Libby started to stroke her best friend's hair as if it might help mend her broken heart.

"I don't know Ell." She paused. "On the one hand, I think fuck him. He doesn't deserve to see you and it I think it will only make you feel worse to see him again when you've made such brave efforts to get over him recently. But on the other hand, I feel like after six years together, you owe it to each other to speak about what happened to your relationship. It might be good for you. It might help you move forwards. But it's hard to know how to advise you if we don't know what he wants to talk about. If he wants to talk about getting back together then that's a totally different problem altogether."

Ella was quiet. "Mmm," she said contemplatively.

"Ella, can I ask you if you still love him?" Libby asked hesitantly.

"Million dollar question eh? I've spent the last year hating him. But I spent six years prior to that loving him." Ella sighed. "I guess the answer is yes. Of course I still love him. It doesn't just go away like that but I resent myself for that. I don't want to love him. I don't think I could ever forgive him for leaving me the way he did. But then, he feels like home. Or he did feel like home. He was my family."

The two women sat silently for a while cuddling against the head of Ella's bed. Libby reached over to the bedside table and turned off the lamp. They lay down in the bed and turned onto their sides, facing each other, both scrunching their arms under the pillow above them.

Ella held Libby's hand and sighed.

The moonlight was shining through the large window and cast an eerie light onto the bed. Libby could see a solitary tear gliding down Ella's face.

Chapter Nine

Ella woke up to see Libby cooking pancakes at the breakfast bar. She sat up and rubbed the sleep from her eyes. She couldn't believe that Libby, of all people, was cooking.

"God, you really must be feeling sorry for me if you are in the *kitchen*!" Ella teased.

"I don't know what you're talking about. I'm a great cook," Libby said, throwing her nose in the air and fluttering her eyelashes. "How are you feeling?"

"Could be better. But okay. Pounding headache," Ella said, searching through her dresser draw for some painkillers.

"Here darling!" Libby charged towards her with a glass of fizzy water that had a disconcerting orange hue to it. She forced it into Ella's reluctant hand and paced back to the bar. "What is it?" Ella asked stroppily.

"Drink it. You're welcome!"

"Mmm," Ella said with sarcasm as she gulped down the concoction in one. "Yummy."

"Vitamin C and Alka Seltzer. Nothing but the best for you madam."

"Thank you," Ella said, clambering out of bed. She pulled up her blinds to reveal a dreary-looking day.

"Now, what are you doing today Miss Successful Artist?"

Ella joined Libby in the kitchen and sat up at the breakfast bar. Libby was grimacing at the batter in the stainless steel mixing bowl. She was using a fork to beat out the lumps that didn't look like they were going anywhere.

Ella walked to the draw on the side of the island and produced a whisk.

"Here. Might be easier." Libby smiled sarcastically.

"You better be hungry! This is exhausting." She sighed. Ella shook her head in despair at her impossibly undomesticated friend. "So go on, what are you doing today Ell?"

"Hmm. I think I'll have lots of things to follow up on after the exhibition. Emails to solidify friendships with the contacts I met last night – that sort of thing. I'm exhibited at the Beat Gallery until the end of January so I need to make sure I advertise things on my end and chase people up – make them invite their friends, their colleagues, their long lost pen pals, their chiropodist, their dogs etc."

"Sounds like a plan! I have to work today at an event. I've got to go and dress some bratty B-list celebrity tonight."

"Gosh. I don't envy you. What event is that for?"

"The premier of some absurdly popular sexy teenage werewolf, vampire, bat film thing. Sweet girl is converted to the dark side by irresistibly attractive but taciturn man who happens to have supernatural powers." Ella raised her eyebrows in disgust. "Just wait, it gets worse. It's a Christmas vampire, werewolf film. The mistletoe has some sort of devilish, seductive power."

Ella cracked up laughing. "Oh Liberty, that sounds positively ghastly. I hope it's a glamorous dress at least."

Libby nodded as she added some butter to the frying pan.

"It might even be worse than seeing your ex-boyfriend!" Ella joked.

"So, you're going to see him then?" Libby asked as she poured the pancake batter into a layer of burnt butter.

Ella shrugged. "I do think we need to see each other. It's just, well I don't know if I want to. Last night as much as I hated him, I just wanted to kiss him." She bit her lip guiltily. "Oh that's so bad for me to admit isn't it?"

"No Ell. It's only natural. You're not a robot; you can't just switch off your *I love Robbie* or *Robbie is so sexy* button. These emotions have gone largely undealt with since you broke up because you haven't seen him."

"Uh huh. But I don't want to give in to any of those feelings. I want to hear what he has to say, ask questions I have about the break-up and then walk away."

Libby was unsure what to say and how best to counsel her friend. Was this an awful mistake going to see Robbie or was he truly sorry for what he had done? They had been a great couple and she had been sure they were going to marry. Now she didn't know what to think. She could only imagine what Ella must be going through.

Libby plonked a dense pancake on Ella's plate. It landed with a loud thud. The two girls looked at each other and burst into a fit of laughter. They could hardly breath and tried desperately to catch their breaths. Ella's laugh was low, a cackle that resonated in the room, and Libby's was a high-pitched frilly laugh; their laughs layered on top of each other sounded ridiculous and this always made them laugh further.

"Oh Libby, do I have to eat that?"

"Yes! Else I'm never bloody cooking for you again!"

"Deal!" Ella cried. She stood off the bar stool and hugged Libby. "Thank you chef. We just need LOADS of toppings and it will be fine!"

The two women raided Ella's cupboard for sweet Christmassy toppings. They opted for Nutella, cinnamon, nutmeg and sliced banana, piling the flavourings high, hoping to mask the taste of the pancakes. They tasted like ash and they were so rubbery they would have been better used as frisbies.

Ella and Libby ate small mouthfuls to stop themselves from choking and they washed them down with a cup of hot tea.

"Shit, these really are awful!" Libby admitted.

"Yupp!" Ella agreed. After nibbling on about a quarter of the pancakes, they threw the rest in the bin and stacked their plates in the washing machine.

"I think I'll also call Fergus today," Ella said. She stood up straight and leant against the sink with her hand on her hips. "He saw Robbie approach me. He went to get us drinks and I have no idea how much of our encounter he saw, I just know he saw, maybe even heard, the end and asked me who he was."

Libby looked concerned. "What do you think he thought of it all?" she asked.

"I don't know. I just said that Robbie was an old friend who had taken me by surprise. I don't want to spoil what I might have with Fergus by pulling Robbie into the equation. Especially when I don't know why he's back all of a sudden."

Libby agreed that it was best not to tell Fergus about who Robbie was and their history together.

Ella thanked Libby for looking after her so well and they said goodbye at Ella's front door.

"Good luck with the werewolves!" Ella cried.

*

It was two o'clock by the time Ella had answered all her emails about the exhibition. Three people had got in touch to ask if she would exhibit at their galleries at some point in the coming year. Andrew Flower from Chase Gallery, Murray Sharp from the new Edinburgh Arts Gallery and Julie Kidman from Shaw Gallery had all expressed an interest in her work. She was delighted with the news and it gave her more courage to face the difficult afternoon that lay ahead of her.

She rang Fergus and they talked merrily about the exhibition. He checked that she was still free on Christmas Eve and told her he had planned a Christmas treat. He knew that this Christmas her brother wasn't around and she would be quite alone on Christmas Eve so he had planned yet another surprise for her. They were going to see the English National Ballet's performance of the *Nutcracker*. It was the perfect Christmas present.

Once she had phoned Fergus, she had to make the call she was dreading. She scrolled down her address book on her iphone and came to the entry 'Robbie Newton'. Ella suddenly wondered if this was still the right number for him. She thought he must have got an American number when he moved to Chicago and had probably discarded the old English one.

Ella wasn't sure if this number would work but she didn't want to contact his family to ask for a current number. It would be too awkward. She took the chance and pressed the dial button. Four solemn rings chimed out and they echoed in her nervous mind. It was now on the sixth ring and she was about to hang up when she heard the line crackle and the sound of Robbie's calm and comforting voice fill the speaker.

"Hello?"

Ella's mouth dried instantly. She couldn't think of what to say. The uncomfortable silence grew until he broke it.

"Helloo?" Another pause.

"Ella, is that you?" he asked excitedly.

"Yes. Yes it's me," she mumbled in return.

"Hi. I'm so glad you rang. I've been trying your mobile all morning. I was beginning to think you were never going to pick up."

"Oh, well, I changed my number about six months ago when I lost my phone," she said, matter of fact. This was bizarre. So much time had passed between them that they didn't even have each other's correct numbers.

"I see. I hope you calling means you will see me tonight? I know you must have reservations about seeing me again but please I need to —"

"Seven o'clock, Trafalgar Square."

"Yes. Yes! Okay, I —"

"Under Nelson's Column. If you are a minute late I'm leaving." Ella hung up the phone. She let out a massive sigh and released all the frantic energy that had bubbled up inside of her. She hadn't planned on saying that but she couldn't bear to be on the phone to him any longer. She knew that Trafalgar Square was a strange place to pick but she wanted to be somewhere surrounded by tourists, somewhere where they could be swamped by the grandeur of London and the impersonality of the surrounding stone. They had no memories there; it was neutral. It was just Trafalgar Square.

*

Robbie was standing under Nelson's Column with a bunch of blush pink peonies. Ella rolled her eyes when she saw them. *Man brings woman favourite flowers. Woman forgives man. Typical, predictable man.* He was going to have to do a lot better than that if he wanted her to stay more than ten minutes. Ella wrapped her scarf a little tighter, pulling it closer to her neck so there were no gaps where the biting cold could seep in against her body. It was frightfully cold, perhaps the coldest day of the year so far and her cream fur coat could only block out the cold so much. She took a deep breath and crossed the square to where Robbie was standing, his face a little in the shadow of the enormous

Christmas tree which was erected in front of the National Gallery.

When Robbie saw Ella walking slowly towards him his face lit up with excitement and relief.

"Hello, Ella my love."

"Please don't call me your love, Robbie. You lost that privilege some time ago."

"These are for you. I feel silly for bringing them now but, well I saw them so often in Chicago on a flower stand or sometimes in the botanical gardens and I thought of you every time I saw them."

You thought of me every time. How considerate of you.

Ella didn't know how to behave; all she could think of were nasty retorts but wasn't she better than that?

She took the flowers and said nothing.

"Shall we walk?"

"Robbie I'd rather we didn't. Can't we just sit on the edge of the fountain and you can say what you want to say and then I can go home."

"Whatever you would like."

They walked over to the fountain on the left hand side of the large statue and stooped to sit down on its edge. Water was still flowing through the feature and the sound of it gushing from the top to the bottom of the fountain blocked out some of the squeals of Italian tourists who were dressed in their puffa-jacket and back-pack uniform. They were angling their cameras and pulling out selfie sticks to take snaps of them climbing the stately lions. Ella turned her attention back to Robbie.

"Ella, I don't know where to start. I made an enormous mistake leaving you in the way I did. I know that it was particularly unforgivable and I want you to know there isn't a day that goes by that I don't berate myself for letting you go and for behaving so atrociously towards you."

Ella said nothing still.

"Being on the other side of the world from you was torture. I didn't want to be in Chicago without you. It's an incredible city but it is nothing without you there. I made a mistake and I want to rectify it."

Ella opened her mouth to speak and then stopped. She thought for a moment. He looked well, too well. His longer hair and slight stubble had transformed his face for the better. She wasn't convinced by his 'heartfelt' confession. He anxiously adjusted his maroon scarf that he had tied too tight.

"It took you almost a whole year to work out you made a mistake?" she asked accusingly.

"No Ella. I knew I had made a mistake as soon as I'd left but I thought I owed it to you to be sure I could give you what you wanted if I came back. I had to be one hundred percent sure that I wanted all the same things as you did before I came charging back into your life. I had to be sure so I didn't inflict any more pain on you."

"While we're on the subject of you charging in, can I just say that you showing up last night was one of the most rude, inconsiderate acts I've ever experienced. Almost on par with leaving me in the first place! It was my first exhibition and I am outraged that you think it was acceptable to barge in there and demand to see me." Ella stopped for a quick breath and then continued: "You talking about how you wanted to be sure, well I was sure. I knew I wanted to be with you for the rest of my life. I was honest with you and you couldn't even give me that same honesty back. You talk as if it's noble of you to have made sure you wanted the same things as me before you came back. Bullshit. You've been a coward. Not once did you call me and tell me any of this. Not once. How do you expect me to believe anything you say now?"

Robbie decided to try a different tact. He had to remind her that she loved him still and that he loved her.

"Didn't you miss me Ell?"

Ella sighed and looked at Robbie straight in the face. There was no point in lying when the truth was so obvious. "Yes, I did," she said soberly.

"Do you still love me?"

Ella looked down at her hands in her lap and played with the edge of her fur coat. He took her hands in his and held them tightly, offering them some much-needed warmth. Ella looked up at him. "How could I love somebody who left me?" she whispered wistfully.

"Oh Ella. I love you so much; I will spend the rest of my life loving you! I will spend the rest of my life making up this year to you! Can we go somewhere inside please? It's doing us no good being out in the cold. Your hands are freezing. I understand why you don't want to go anywhere with me but there's still so much to say and you are going to freeze your beautiful bottom off if we sit here any longer." He added the last comment with a cheeky chin. Ella had to hold back a smile. Robbie had always been obsessed with her bottom. When he saw that the comment momentarily melted her icy front he knew he couldn't waste the opportunity. He needed to remind her how well he knew her, how good they were together. After all, he had knowledge of all her favourite theatres, restaurants, and landmarks on his side. That had to count for something.

"Let's go and eat at *Sarastro*. Do you still love that place?"

Ella nodded involuntarily.

They walked to Drury Lane in silence. They took it in turns to look at one another and then sheepishly turn the other way when they were caught out.

When they got to the restaurant, they were seated in a booth that was tucked away from other dinners. *Sarastro* was designed for after theatre dining; it described itself as *the show after the show*. The walls were lined with glittering props like Venetian masks and were painted with exuberant colours. The gold ceilings were adorned with low hanging lampshades and exotic music was being played live. Stepping inside was like stepping into an endless treasure cave of collected Venetian trinkets, or like walking onto the set of Phantom of the Opera. Ella, was glad that the maître d' had placed them in a relatively intimate booth; she was thinking about the possibility of raising her voice with Robbie and she didn't want it to be awkward if any other dinners were too close.

"You know, I've pictured your face every night before I go to sleep. But you are so much more striking in the flesh," Robbie said, once they had sat down.

"Well I pictured your face every night and mentally stuck pins in it," Ella said, the words escaping her before she had even noticed. "Sorry, that sounded gauche didn't it? But as you can imagine, my thoughts about you haven't exactly been very positive recently and I shouldn't be the one apologising actually."

"No, that's fair enough."

"So tell me Robbie, what was your new girlfriend like? You didn't fancy bringing her back to England with you?" Ella asked with spite.

Robbie was shocked.

"I can see from your face that you didn't think I knew about your yank. Word travels fast, even across the Atlantic Robert."

Robert? Nobody but his mother calls him Robert! Ella knew she was angry with him but saying Robert sounded so strange on her tongue. They had never been that formal together before. He had always been Robbie, *her* Robbie.

"Ella you must know that was just a distraction from the heartbreak," he said as he pulled the menu towards him, pretending to read it.

"Mmhm and did that distraction help you figure out if you *wanted the same things as me*?" she said quoting the words he used earlier.

He put the menu down. "Ella," he said softly. "I can see how much I've hurt you and I'm sorry. The woman you're referring to was never my girlfriend. She was just the tiniest of flings and it meant nothing. And yes, dating someone that wasn't you did help me realise that I wanted the same things as you so …"

Her icy stare was back.

"Ella, you know I hate Americans! It was never anything serious!" he said trying to lighten the mood.

Just then, the waiter came over and recited the specials in his very best English accent. He smelt of salty onions and duck fat and he looked like he had used a little chip oil to slick back his greasy hair.

Ella ordered the *Confit de Canard*, not put off by his *odour de duck*, and Robbie ordered the Beef Bourguignon and a bottle of Rioja to accompany their meaty dishy. Robbie was very good with wine. Regrettably, it was one of his many talents.

Before they had time to strike up the conversation again, the waiter had come back with their wine. He poured them two large glasses and Ella reminded herself not to drink too much, to stay in control.

It was Ella who spoke when the waiter left. She told Robbie what it was like when he had left her and how difficult it had been selling the house they owned together without him. She had liaised with his brother and the whole operation had been a nightmare. Robbie sat silently for the best part of forty minutes, listening patiently to Ella.

"The first six months were ghastly, the worst of my life. But, slowly the pain dulled and after six months the numbness disappeared. I started to do things for myself. I buried myself in my art and I bought my own flat."

"Ella, that's great you bought a house."

"And now I'm seeing someone."

"Oh." There was a long awkward pause as Robbie digested the unwelcomed news. "How long have you been together?" he asked finally.

Ella winced at the prospect of telling the truth. One week would sound ridiculous if she said it out loud but she liked Fergus so much that saying *one week* didn't do their relationship justice.

"A while," she replied. "He was at the exhibition." They both took a swig of their wine and Ella realised that they had finished a bottle already. The main course still hadn't come and Ella was starting to feel tipsy.

Robbie called over the waiter and politely inquired as to the whereabouts of their food, no doubt distracting himself from the topic at hand. He ordered another bottle of wine and turned back to Ella.

"Well, I'd like to say I'm happy for you." Ella scrunched up her mouth and squinted her eyes critically. "But, I wouldn't mean it. *I* want to be with you."

"It's always about what *you* want."

"Ella, I need to tell you more about the lead up to my decision to leave. That's why I wanted to see you tonight. I wanted to apologise, then explain and then, well, we'll get to the other reason later." He edged a little closer to her in the booth so they were no longer on different edges of the table opposite each other but were on the same side, sitting side by side on the leather seat. Ella winced a little as he drew closer. Her physical reaction to his proximity didn't go unnoticed but it was ignored. Robbie moved closer again and she could smell the fragrance of his Hugo Boss cologne. The scent filled her nose and reminded her of Italy, the Alps, the fishing village in Cornwall — all the places they had holidayed together.

She pushed these thoughts to the back of her mind and took a swig of the wine the waiter had just come over to pour.

She was flirting with the dangerous side of tipsy but she was not going to stop drinking now. She needed the wine glass to act as a prop, a distraction and focus point to keep her from looking into Robbie's hazel eyes.

"Ella, last Christmas I was planning to propose to you."

Ella's jaw dropped to the floor. She didn't believe him. Was this a ploy to get her back?

"You remember the silver bracelet I gave you that had diamonds and sapphires on it?" Ella nodded silently, scared to hear what he was going to say next. "Well that was meant to be Part One of the present. Part Two was an engagement ring I was going to give to you on Christmas Day but when it came down to it ..." It was his turn to break for wine now. He took a massive gulp and continued when he saw the panic in Ella's face.

"I had decided to propose to you a few months before December, October maybe, and I was going to do it on Christmas morning in bed after you opened your stocking. But a few weeks before, doubts crept in. I started to panic about being too young, about not being ready and then it seemed everywhere I went, everyone was talking about marriage and why not to do it! You started to allude to it a lot and while I know you did so in jest and sweetly, every little mention of it started to weigh me down a little bit more."

Ella couldn't believe what her ex-boyfriend was telling her. So she had been right. She had seen the signs and she hadn't been making the whole thing up in her head!

She could feel the full effect of the alcohol now. She felt that the volume of wine she had just consumed was about to flow straight out of her eyes.

Ella felt a tear escape her right eye and she saw Robbie move to wipe it for her. His hand lingered on her face and he tucked one of her curls behind her ear.

"Don't," she whispered.

He was so close she could feel his warm breath on her cheek.

"My darling Ella. I was a fool not to go through with it. I should never have listened to anybody else. I should have ignored their prejudiced and biased comments about how marriage changed everything. But, I'm here now.

"I want to spend the rest of my life with you. I will spend the rest of my days making up what I did to you, I promise."

Ella was a wreck. She was crying profusely and looking from Robbie's eyes to the floor and back again. Finally he was saying all the things she had hoped to hear for so long. For months after he left she had imagined him storming back through their front door and telling her he made a mistake. He *wanted* her, he *loved* her. Now it was actually happening and she didn't know what to do. He was looking longingly at her and started to push the table away from them slightly.

Ella didn't know why he was creating a gap between the table and the leather seat but when he dropped onto one knee she understood instantly. He took out a small box from his pocket and opened it. There starring at her was an elegant ring with spectacular diamonds sitting either side of an enormous sapphire. It matched the bracelet he had given her last Christmas.

She was lost for words. She felt a lump in her throat rising and all parts of her body screamed different things to her. *No. Yes. No. Yes.*

"Ella Moore, will you marry me? This is something I should have asked you a long time ago.

I love you endlessly and there would be no greater pleasure in life than being your husband."

Ella was still in shock. She was shaking her head from left to right in disbelief. Robbie wasn't sure if she was saying no or if she was just overwhelmed by the situation. He took the ring from the box, slid it onto her ring finger and sat back down next to her. He sat so close to her that his soft lips were brushing her face. Ella looked at him with confusion and he kissed her. His lips were just as she had remembered them; cool, smooth and oh so familiar. She felt her heart ache as he pressed against her lips. She kissed him passionately for a moment, but although she had dreamt of this for so long, something niggled at her. Something felt strange and she drew back from him. Their kiss had felt bizarre and Ella was now wracked with guilt.

What was she doing? She didn't want this. She suddenly realised that she didn't feel the same for Robbie anymore. She didn't want him. She wanted Fergus. She wanted to run home and find Fergus waiting for her. She stood up suddenly.

"Robbie," she said sternly. "I cannot marry you."

Robbie's face flooded with panic as she took off the ring and laid it on the table. She slid clumsily between the table and the seat until she was freed of the booth. She turned to look at him, this gorgeous man who had once been the love of her life but was now the love of her past.

"I will never marry you. You are one year too late Robbie."

She turned her back on him and headed to the door, noticing on her way the waiter carrying a Beef Bourguignon and a *Confit de Canard* in the direction of their table. Her walk turned into a jog and she sped quickly through the restaurant until she was in the street. She ran all the way to the nearest tube station in her heels, feeling liberated by what had just happened. She sat down on the underground seat and began to laugh.

Chapter Ten

Ella was brushing her teeth in the bathroom when the sound of the kettle startled her. She had forgotten she had put it on and now its screeching was trying to win her attention. She slid aside the glass door of the bathroom and rushed to the hob to take the kettle off the flame. She poured the boiling water onto her teabag and went back to the bathroom to spit out the foamy toothpaste that had collected in her mouth.

Ella slipped on a pair of jeans and a charcoal grey cashmere jumper that was soft and flattered her waist. Once she was dressed she added a dash of milk to her earl grey and stared into the rippling brown hot liquid.

What was she going to do today? She sipped the tea and thought about how she could fill her lazy Sunday. She didn't want to brave the cold but she wanted to do something Christmassy. Perhaps it was the perfect day to watch festive films she thought; Christmas Day was only two days away now and she could do with relaxing after the busy week she'd had. Suddenly Ella remembered presents! She hadn't yet wrapped any of the ones she had bought. She took her tea into the art studio where all the gifts, paper, scissors and ribbon were stored.

Sitting in the studio, Ella realised how strange it looked now that her paintings were not there. This empty space was normally so full of colour and life and although the exposed redbrick walls looked rustic and pretty, the room felt bare. She couldn't help but feel the barrenness of the room reflected her glum state. Although she felt she had made the right decision with regards to Robbie, she still felt a pang of loneliness. Every time she folded the blue-glitter-encrusted silver wrapping paper, a loud crunching sound was produced and echoed against the naked walls. Ella tried to remind herself that this noise was not one of emptiness or loneliness but in fact, it was the sound of success. The amplified sound was only heard because her paintings were being exhibited and all of them had been bought!

But Ella's thoughts drifted back to the night before. She couldn't believe that Robbie had proposed to her. She wondered if he had been planning on returning and asking her to marry him for a while or if it had just been a spur of the moment thing in the lead up to Christmas. Ella's thoughts strayed from Robbie to Fergus. She felt so guilty for having kissed Robbie, even momentarily, when she and Fergus were an item, or they were about to be an item. But she was also glad that she had kissed Robbie because it had given her the closure she needed and shown how just what she had with Fergus. Last night's kiss had felt foreign and uncanny but her first kiss with Fergus on that patio … wow. She knew it was clichéd but when he had kissed her she had felt like a firework had exploded inside her.

Ella's contemplation was interrupted by a knock on the door. Ella wasn't sure who it could be; she wasn't expecting anybody and it was a Sunday so it couldn't be the postman. She stood up and opened the heavy metal door to see Harry, Charlie, Lara and Libby all huddled for warmth like a pack of penguins braving the icy wind.

"Hi! What a surprise! Come in!" she said, welcoming them.

"We come bearing gifts!" Harry grinned as he stepped over the threshold and gestured to a large bag of goodies.

"We thought we'd cook you a roast. Cheer you up a bit and celebrate the exhibition of course!" Lara said, taking off her jacket and settling a large hessian bag of food on the breakfast bar.

"Oh guys, you shouldn't have!" Ella cried, so happy to see her friends. "I hope Libby's not cooking though!"

"Ha ha ha," Libby said sarcastically. "No, I'm in charge of entertainment. I'll do the music. I knew you were in today, I hope you don't mind we came over," she said as she walked over to Ella's stereo.

"It's a wonderful surprise."

The group gathered around the kitchen island and unpacked the supplies while they listened to Michael Bublé's hit Christmas album.

They spent the early afternoon marinating the beef and peeling the potatoes. When the spuds were parboiled they squished each one a little and doused them in goose fat before putting them into the oven to roast alongside the meat. The veggies were sliced and the Yorkshire puddings were defrosted.

"We're cheating on the Yorkshire's – just Aunt Bessie's!" Lara explained.

"But we did buy a rather nice bottle of Cabernet Sauvignon which will more than make up for ready-made Yorkshires," Harry said, as he poured Ella a glass and forced her to sit down and relax. Ella was so happy to see her best friends teetering around her, preparing wonderful smelling Christmas fare. She decided that they should set up a dinning table in her art studio as there was ample space now and only room for two people at the breakfast bar.

Harry and Charlie hopped to it and moved one of Ella's desks that was pressed up against the wall into the centre of the room. They flung a red tablecloth over the desk that Ella had lying around. They added the plates, cutlery and Christmas crackers to the table and for every item they placed down, Libby adjusted it. She rearranged the mistletoe and candles to look more elegant and also to prevent the plant catching fire on the flames. Watching them set the table was like watching a ballet sequence from the *Nutcracker*; they navigated their way around each other, turning and swirling with poise, all moving to the same rhythm.

As the men completed the final movement of their dance, the *fetch the napkins* sequence, Lara and Libby brought in the piping hot food.

No sooner had they sat down to feast, than the questions about last night were asked.

"So, how was it last night?" Lara asked. "Libby told us you met with *you know who* but that she couldn't come to see you afterwards because the pre-teen diva she had to dress was causing a scene."

"Mm," Libby said, swallowing her sip of wine. "She was *so* drunk that she ran around trying to take her clothes off at the after party. I had to keep redressing her!"

"But back to the question …" Lara interrupted.

Ella told her closest friends all about the evening she had had. She told them how she had chosen somewhere neutral for them to meet so that she could keep her distance and that Robbie had thought that he could woo her by taking her to one of her *old* favourite restaurants. She told them that she had started off cold and resolute but with the help of a little wine and Robbie's charm she had opened up a little more and grown more affectionate. Finally, she told them that he had proposed.

"He proposed!?" Charlie asked, as he spat out a little of his wine, clearly mortified.

"Shit," said Harry.

"Wow!" said Lara.

"What a head fuck," said Libby. "How on earth did you react?"

"I said no, obviously."

Libby sighed a huge sigh of relief and Charlie slammed his hand on the table in pleasure.

Ella paused for a while, waiting on Lara and Harry's reactions. "I said no and then I ran out of the restaurant and I haven't spoken to him since," she continued.

"Well done you!" Libby said, practically whooping. "Doesn't he know it's not just about the proposal anymore? Urgh, he doesn't understand that he changed things by going away. *Men.*"

"Exactly Libs, he doesn't understand that at all. Although it was a pretty horrid conversation, I did enjoy seeing the look on his face when I said no!" she admitted. Charlie who was sitting opposite her at the other head of the table grinned with her. It reminded her that she still wasn't sure if Charlie had caught up with Robbie on the night of the exhibition and said something to him. She wouldn't be surprised if he had and she would ask him after supper.

Ella turned to Lara now who had been quiet ever since Ella had them told them she had turned Robbie down.

"What is it?" Ella demanded.

Lara looked up at Ella and shifted in her seat. She placed her knife and fork down and started to speak.

"Well, don't bite my *head* off but I assumed you'd *have* said yes. It is what you have wanted for so *long*, to have a family and a future with him. And now *he* is offering it to you. I'm not *saying* you should forgive him straight away for *what* he did but I'm surprised you said no to marrying him."

Suddenly the four friends were off, each battling to voice their opinions. Charlie and Libby disagreed with Lara; they didn't think Robbie deserved Ella after what he had done. But Harry agreed with Lara and said that Ella shouldn't be stubborn, she should appreciate that Robbie had the courage to admit that he had made a mistake and was coming back to fix it like a man. Their bickering went on for a few minutes until Ella stood up suddenly.

"Guys!" she shouted. "I have made my decision. I am resolute. I appreciate your support, your love, and your advice. You've all been incredible this last year but this is my decision and I'd like you to respect it. I do not want to marry Robbie."

She sat down and they all nodded obediently.

Lara spoke first. "We only want the *best* for you *Ell*. I didn't mean to —"

"I know," Ella said smiling as she put her hand on Lara's. "And this *is* best for me. I can see things I hadn't seen before. Robbie and I weren't right and I feel really strongly about Fergus." The others raised their eyebrows as they finished the remains of their meal and Ella continued. "I really like Fergus. I know it's so soon to say but, well I feel so different when I am with him. I feel like a bolder, more courageous and better version of myself when I'm with him. He's the most thoughtful man I've ever met and I think I'd be daft not to see where it goes. Just the way he looks at me …" Ella trailed off and noticed her friends were giggling.

"What? What is it?" she asked.

"Nothing," Harry said, laughing. "It's just you put on this weird dreamy voice when you talk about Fergus."

"No I do not!"

"Yes you do!" they all cried.

"Ella's iiinnn looorrveee," Charlie teased.

Using her spoon, Ella catapulted a big chunk of carrot at Charlie's face.

"You guys are so ridiculous. One minute you are arguing about whether I should get married to my ex-boyfriend and then the next you are claiming I'm in love with a man I've only known for a week!" There was an eruption of laughter and they began to sling bits of food at each other across the table.

"Ha ha. Exasperating aren't we? Aren't you so glad you have us!?" Libby asked Ella, as she flung a spoonful of peas at her.

"Yes actually! I'm so lucky!" she cried as she flicked a roast potato back at Libby.

"Let's get this cleaned up and bring out pudding before we end up getting beef on the ceiling!" Lara said quickly, keen to avoid a full-blown food fight which would ruin her white jumper.

While everybody emptied the table and prepared the decadent-looking Marks & Spencer sticky toffee pudding, Ella checked her phone. Thirty-seven missed calls from Robbie Newton and a text from Fergus: *So looking forward to seeing you tomorrow night. Let's dress black tie and go somewhere lovely afterwards. Shall I pick you up at 6.30pm? x*

Ella replied, confirming her excitement and the time and remembered that she needed to pick up her fur jacket that she forgot to pick up as she was running out of *Sarastro* on Saturday evening. She would wear it tomorrow night on Christmas Eve with one of her full-length dresses, though she wasn't sure which one.

She turned her phone off and went back to her friends who were now helping themselves to a glass of port. They finished the scrumptious pudding and exchanged presents under the small tree that Ella had bought and decorated a few weeks ago. Overcome by sleepiness and an indulgently full feeling, they all flopped onto Ella's sofa and began to watch *It's a Wonderful Life*.

Chapter Eleven

It was Christmas Eve and Ella was feeling exceptionally festive. She had spent the day with Libby wandering around Christmas markets and sampling Christmas treats. They had gone to Winter Wonderland and gorged on German pretzels, yellow and pink striped hard candies, crepes and a lot of mulled wine. They had been wrapped up in cosy bobble hats and gloves when snow started to fall. There was a light wind so the snowflakes fluttered up and down, swirling in the air like butterflies. It hadn't snowed since Friday morning when she had stayed the night at Fergus' for the first time. That night had been so incredible that she hoped she would be spending this night with him again. She told Libby about the ballet that her and Fergus were going to and that they had planed to wear black tie. Ella ran through her dress options with Libby, her personal stylist, who insisted that she should wear her red silk dress because it was both knockout and fantastically festive.

The two best friends had been walking through the rosy-cheeked crowds at Winter Wonderland arm in arm for over an hour. They had spent their time talking about men, fashion and work. Libby told Ella she had met someone at the premiere on

Saturday evening. He was a red-headed actor who had boldly, but smoothly, asked her for her number. She had given it to him happily and had spent most of the after party laughing with him, (when she wasn't dressing her ward).

Ella was ecstatic to hear that Libby had a new love interest and hinted at a double date with her and Fergus if things became more serious with this Eddie.

They had eaten so much throughout the day that Ella had no idea how she was going to fit into her dress now that she was at home looking at it in the flesh. She stared at it on the bed, the scarlet silk shining brightly against her cream bedspread. Ella knew that there was only one way to hold in her sweetie-bloated stomach and that was spanks. She said a little prayer for the person who had invented the nifty creation and hoisted them up above her waist.

She slipped on her silk dress. It was simple, elegant and sexy. It had two thin shoulder straps that criss-crossed over her back. At the base of the spine the material gathered and scooped low so that her whole back was exposed. The neckline at the front showed a hint of cleavage but the main focus of the dress was the devastatingly seductive slit that run up her left leg. It wasn't a very warm outfit to be wearing on a snowy night but she had her fur coat, that she had collected from the restaurant before going to meet Libby. Going back to *Sarastro* where Robbie had proposed hadn't brought back as many emotions as she had thought it would and Ella was proud of herself for staying strong and for refusing to pick up any of Robbie's calls, even when he had started to ring every half an hour.

Ella adjusted her dress under her bust and slid the material a little to the right as the leg slit had encouraged the dress to swim westerly across her body. She heard a car pull up outside her flat so she picked up her cream clutch bag and went outside to meet Fergus.

Fergus greeted her with a gentle kiss on the lips and the connection made her feel electric. They headed off in a taxi and talked about their weekends, though Ella was careful not to mention what she did on Saturday night. They drove past Trafalgar square, Charing Cross station and on to St Martin's Lane where the cab stopped.

When they stepped into the London Coliseum they turned heads; they were without a doubt the most glamorous couple in there, though other people had dressed up smartly for the Christmas Eve show. Fergus collected their tickets from the box office while Ella took in the theatre's grand surroundings.

Ella was feasting on the ornate ceiling when a buzzing in her clutch interrupted her. Her phone was on silent but it was still vibrating. She reached into the sequined cream purse and turned off the vibrate settings on her mobile. She couldn't deal with Robbie's persistent pestering. Her phone was exhausted from the relentless ringing and all she wanted to do was drop it on the floor so that it would be swept into a crowd of expensively heeled shoes. She resisted the urge to drop her phone on the floor but she did finally give in to temptation of her voicemail. She dialled in and listened to the first of three messages:

"Ell, please tark to me. Pleease pick up, I love yyou." Robbie was drunk. He mumbled something incomprehensible and then she heard what she thought was "need to seez you t'night." She hung up the voicemail and turned her phone off. The silent setting wasn't enough; she wanted her and Fergus to have a wonderful evening together without Robbie haunting her mailbox or her mind. She crammed her phone into her bag in exasperation just as Fergus returned with the tickets.

Ella followed Fergus up the lefthand staircase to a private box. She was thrilled that they would be sitting in their own secluded balcony, with a personal waiter and a superior view. Ella wondered how Fergus was able to book all of these wonderful treats at such short notice. Alice's Underground Adventures, the Planetarium and now the *Nutcracker* in a box! All of these events had to be booked well in advance which led her to believe that he must very well connected.

As the curtain began to draw apart and the house lights dimmed, Fergus and Ella moved their chairs a little closer to each other. The thick velvet drapes parted to reveal a dreamland of glittering white forests as the music began to stir. The brilliant red uniforms of the toy soldiers stood in contrast to the snow-encrusted woodlands and the dark green of the colossus pine tree that dwarfed the stage.

Fergus looked over to see pure delight lighting up Ella's face.

*

After the show, Ella and Fergus went to a speakeasy around the corner from the theatre. They sipped on delicious cocktails and spoke about the performance. They were peckish after a long stint of drinking but they didn't want to let the snow thicken too much before heading home. They searched for a taxi while eating soggy chips from a polystyrene box. They wondered how funny they must look ambling through the West End in glamorous black tie diving into a box of greasy chips in the middle of the snowy street.

They finally hopped in a cab and headed to Ella's flat.

As the taxi pulled up, Ella took out her purse and paid the driver making it clear that they were both getting out at her flat.

Ella unlocked the door and stumbled through the steel frame. She switched on a few side lamps that brought a warm glow to the studio.

"Ella, this studio is so cool. It's got so much character!"

She thanked him and gave him the grand tour showing him her art space behind the wall at the head of her bed.

"I love it! So great you can paint here too," Fergus said. "It's very you."

"And what does that mean?" Ella asked cheekily, drawing closer to him.

"Well, sophisticated, beautiful, creative, unique," he said as he stroked her cheek. He leant in and kissed the arch of her neck, sending tingles down her spine. He kissed her lightly up her neck, across her jaw line and up to her lips. He lingered for a moment and then kissed her again as he started to pull off her heavy coat.

She took it off completely and led him back through to her living area.

"Would you like some wine?" she asked, her voice slightly raspy now.

"Tell me where it is and I'll pour us some," he replied smiling. She put her coat on the bed and showed him her small collection of wine in the rack standing against the side of the kitchen island.

He decided on a Merlot and poured them two large glasses. Ella slipped off her silver heels and walked back over to the island looking sultry as she moved. It was hard not to walk sexily in her red dress as the slit was so provocative. Fergus couldn't help but grin at how irresistible she looked and he raised his glass for a toast.

"To meeting you just in time for Christmas," he said as his eyes sparkled.

Ella pouted and raised her eyebrows at the sentimental toast.

"To Christmas and," she paused thoughtfully, "to the most magical ten days with you." They clinked glasses and sipped their wine, not taking their eyes off each other.

As they put their glasses down on the table there was a mighty knock at the door, which made them jump. Ella spilled some wine on the counter as the aggressive metallic knock had taken her by surprise. They looked at each other both a little perturbed as to who would be knocking on Christmas Eve so late. The rapping started again, louder this time.

Ella walked to the front door and unlocked the door. Robbie was leaning against the doorframe, one hand on his hip and his breath crisp on the cold air.

Ella's face dropped. Panic spread across her body as she took in the inebriated Robbie standing square in front of her.

"Ella, who is it? Is everything okay?" Fergus asked as he saw Ella's body freeze from behind.

Robbie pushed over the front door and walked into the room.

"Ella, Ella …" He was stumbling, his red eyes trying to focus on his ex-girlfriend.

"Robbie what are you doing here?" she shouted, mortified at his presence.

Fergus moved around the island realising that this man was the tall figure that had shown up at Ella's exhibition.

"Ella, I had to see you. You wouldn't answer your phone."

"Robbie, there is a reason I didn't answer my phone and you know it. I'd like you to leave." Ella could feel Fergus' gaze was on the pair of them and she didn't know what to do.

"So, yourr saying Zaturday meant nothing?" he asked slurring.

Ella was determined not to let Robbie destroy the evening or say something that might upset Fergus.

"No. Please leave."

"Yourr sayin' our kiss meant nothing?"

"You kissed this guy?" Fergus asked gently but with disdain.

Ella turned to explain but Robbie got there first.

"Yess. And this *guy*," he said gesturing to himself, "is Ella's boyfriend of six years."

"*Ex*-boyfriend," Ella said bitterly, snapping back to Robbie's direction.

"Ella, I asskd you to marry me and I'll do it again now," he said. As he attempted to bend down onto one knee, Robbie lost his footing and fell. He hit his head on the edge of her wooden bed and clutched it as it had started to bleed. Ella rushed to his rescue.

"Are you okay?" she asked, inspecting his cut.

"I'm fine," he said, steadying himself. He got back onto one knee now and was searching for something in his pockets.

"Look Ella, you wanted to marry me, whatz changed?"

Ella stood up to talk to Fergus. She wanted, no she needed, to salvage this quickly otherwise he was going to draw the wrong conclusions and think the worst of her.

"Fergus, I —"

"I think I better leave," he said staring solemnly at Ella. She was tongue-tied and didn't know how to explain Robbie's appearance, the kiss and the proposal all in one go. She shook her head flustered and tried to speak again.

"Fergus, please —"

"No Ella, I think you two clearly need to talk." He walked across the room and picked up his coat. He turned back to see Ella glued to the same spot opposite the man who was wobbling absurdly down on one knee.

"So long as he's not too drunk that you feel unsafe … I'll be going."

Ella swallowed. Of course she didn't feel unsafe, it was Robbie. She gave a light nod, thinking it best for her to deal with Robbie alone.

Fergus looked down at her and said "goodbye Ella" with an unsettling finality. His eyes looked full of disappointment. He left swiftly, the metallic shrillness of the door reinforcing Ella's new feeling of emptiness.

She sighed and looked at her drunken ex-boyfriend. He was falling asleep, one hand clutching the ring he had finally found, and the other supporting himself against the floor. His head was bobbing down to meet his cocked leg and he was dribbling.

Chapter Twelve

Ella woke up to the sound of Robbie's grunting snore. It bellowed through the room and pierced the festive air like a pneumatic drill. It was Christmas Day and Ella awoke to see her ex-boyfriend slumped over her sofa like a stocking that was yet to be filled.

She got out of bed, showered and changed in the bathroom. She walked over to the source of the stale smell of alcohol and sat down next to him.

Robbie stirred slightly, his eyes opening, hazy at first but when he realised he was looking up at Ella's stern face, he rubbed his eyes and bolted upright. He looked up at her like a school child waiting to be reprimanded by his head master.

"Merry Christmas," Ella said with quiet sarcasm.

"Oh Ella, it's Christmas Day and I've ruined it for you."

Ella said nothing.

"What happened?" Robbie asked, a nervous weak smile twitching across his face.

"You don't remember?" Ella said surprised. She had to fight the urge to be rude.

He shook his head in shame.

"Well, let's see. You barged in here drunk interrupting my Christmas Eve date, you proceeded to tell the man that I'm dating that we kissed the other day and proposed to me again, this time in front of him. Then you practically passed out while still down on one knee and I had to drag you to the sofa."

Robbie winced.

"Ella, I know you're tired of hearing it, and it sounds so mechanically devoid of meaning now that I've said it so many times, but please know I am sorry."

She nodded, acknowledging his apology and stared up at the ceiling.

"I have handled this all so badly. I thought I could come back and solve this but I can see I was wrong. You have moved on and I need to respect that. I need to accept that. You seem to be doing so well, brilliant even. Oh, that sounds patronising when I didn't mean it to be. I just meant that you look great, exceptional, at the moment. I know I have a funny way of showing it but I'm so happy for you that your career is sky-rocketing too."

"Thank you, Robbie."

They sat in silence for some time until Robbie spoke finally.

"I can't believe I've lost the most wonderful thing I ever had."

It was Ella's turn to wince now. How did one answer that?

"Well, maybe we haven't lost anything. Maybe we can still be friends in the future," Ella said half-heartedly. They looked at each other, recognising that this would never happen.

"I wish that could be true Ella. But I don't think it can be with our history, not for a long time anyway. It would never be simple because I've really screwed this up!"

They laughed a little and talked for a few minutes about their relationship and about how they would both move forwards without each other. Robbie was back in London for good but he promised he would give her space.

Ella took his hand in hers. "I did love you an awful amount and we did have a fantastic relationship Robbie."

"We had fun, didn't we?" he asked.

"Yes, but we argued."

"All the time. We could never —"

"Agree on anything! I'm surprised we managed to buy a house together."

"Or choose where to go on holiday."

"We had so many holidays."

"We had so much sex!"

Ella laughed a little now, remembering fondly that Robbie always tried to sprinkle humour into serious conversations. He hadn't been wrong in what he had said though – they had shared an undeniably strong chemistry.

"Yes. We did. We always agreed when it came to that ..." Ella admitted. She pulled her hand away and straightened up, tugging down her dress that had ridden up her leg.

"Ella?"

"Yes, Robbie?"

"Merry Christmas." Robbie said it with sadness heavy in his eyes. He stood up to go but he put his hands on either side of her cheeks and leant down to kiss her forehead. She closed her eyes as he did so, soaking up the last of her past.

"One thing before you go ..." she asked.

"Anything," he said tenderly.

"How did you know where I lived?"

Robbie sighed self-consciously, embarrassed to admit how he knew.

"I text Jimi. I asked him where your new house was. I said it was urgent."

Ella shook her head in disbelief. She walked towards him and hugged him and held him tightly in an embrace that lasted for a minute or two.

"Goodbye Robbie," she said finally as she closed the door behind him.

*

"Libby! I can't come for lunch. I'm so sorry, but I was with Fergus last night and Robbie showed up. He spoke about a kiss and marrying me and Fergus ran off and he won't answer any of my calls. I have to go and find him and explain," she rambled.

"Oh my god, darling! Shit, breathe! Christmas drama! Oh crap, *Merry Christmas*! Listen, don't worry. Emily's just gone into labour so I think we'll be missing Christmas lunch too!"

"Ahhh!!!! Why didn't you say?"

"I'm going to be an auntie!" she screeched.

"How exciting! Oh send them my love please. Call me when she's born and tell Toby he's going to be a wonderful father!"

"Will do! Good luck with Fergus. Go and get him! Hopefully we'll still host Boxing Day tomorrow so I'll see you then?"

"Of course. Let's talk later when things have calmed down on both of our ends! But Libs, before you go, you don't have Fergus' home address to you? His parents' home address? He said he was driving to theirs this morning and I just need to see him. I need to explain everything otherwise he's going to think I'm the worst human being in the world. Is it okay to go to his house? Is it too bold?"

"It's the perfect amount of bold. It's bloody Christmas Day and romantic — you *have* to do it! I'll find the address and text it you in a second; we're just heading to the hospital. Eeek!! Good luck!!"

"And to you Auntie Libby!"

Libby was going to be an auntie and Ella was going to go after Fergus!

Was this mad? Libby thought. What did she need? She packed her handbag, slid a pair of dark chocolate suede knee high boots over her tights and grabbed her cream hat and matching scarf.

Her phone pinged. She was disappointed to find it wasn't Libby with Fergus' address but she was happy to see the message was from Jimi.

Hey baby sis, Merry Christmas! Is everything okay? Robbie text me yesterday and asked for your address ... is he back? Are you two back together? Tell me what's going on! Having breakfast by myself in the hotel – most depressing Christmas ever! Hope your morning is better than mine. Will call later, you're probably still asleep. Lots of love, J x

She shot him a quick reply telling him not to worry and that she would explain all when he was home on New Year's Eve. Just as she put her phone down, it pinged again, this time with the coveted address. She put the address into her phones' GPS app. It was a small village in Hampshire just under two hours away. With nobody driving on Christmas Day, everybody tucked up in their cosy homes surely the roads would be empty? She could get there in no time.

Ella picked up her things, locked the house and de-frosted her windscreen. She jumped in the car, put her bag on the passenger seat, wedged her phone into the slot under the heaters that didn't work, and turned the key. The steering wheel was cold in her hands and she lamented the lack of warmth. She meant to get her heating fixed before winter but she had never found the time. She turned on the radio as she merged onto the A1 and then onto the M4. Ten minutes into her journey, on the outskirts of London, light snow began to fall. As the tall grey buildings of London turned into green fields and idyllic cottages, the snow thickened all around her.

Ella started to think seriously for the first time about what she was doing.

Was this an absolutely crazy idea? Storming Fergus' house uninvited on Christmas Day? When she thought about it like that, of course it was. But Fergus was ignoring her calls since Robbie had burst in on them and she had no choice. She had to make it right with him. Ella coughed as the biting cold infiltrated every limb of her body. She could see her breath on the inside of her car and she pulled her bobble hat tighter over her face to retain as much heat as possible. She listened to Christmas Carols that were playing on the radio and sang along to keep herself warm.

Ella looked out the windscreen to see signs for Andover and was suddenly plagued with doubt. She was getting close. What was she going to say? How was she going to explain her and Robbie's past and his intrusion last night and what was Fergus going to say in return? She really hadn't thought this through properly and her building anxiety distracted her from concentrating on the road. *What did that sign just say?* She squinted at the next sign but it didn't say anything about the upcoming junction - it was just a sign for the next services.

A junction was approaching and Ella didn't know whether she was meant to take the exit or continue on the road. She quickly consulted her phone map again and it advised her to take the exit onto a small B road. She took the exit but noticed that her battery was down to 7% - the GPS app was draining all her battery. She urged it to survive just twenty more minutes.

Ella drove on, following the automated directions. The countryside was becoming increasingly wild and the snow was piled up on the sides of the road almost a metre thick.

Ella turned down a small lane that her phone prompted her to take. She looked at the next set of directions just in case her phone ran out of battery before she had got to Fergus' house. The map told her to stay on this road for three miles and then turn left immediately after a bridge and then right again into what looked like a private road.

Ella could no longer feel her feet but she persevered. The snow on the side lane looked treacherously thick so she slowed down to avoid skidding.

Just as she navigated her way gently around a bend a large popping noise made her jump in her seat. The pop was followed by a slight hiss and as she rolled forward she felt the car growing heavier. Ella tried to accelerate a little but she felt the car lagging. She looked in her rear view mirror and realised that her view was slopping down to the left and the car was wonky.

She stopped the car and went to assess the damage. Her back left tyre was flat. Just her luck! Ella traipsed back a few metres down the quiet road to see what had caused the puncture. She saw a brown lump in the snow and dusted the snow away to find a small cog that looked like it belonged to a tractor or a snowplough. She picked it up and felt the rough and rusting grooves of the cog in her hand. What was she going to do now? She had never changed a tyre before and she wasn't even sure if she had a spare one to swap the old one with. She was stuck in the middle of nowhere and no one knew where she was.

Ella decided she'd try to get through to Fergus once more and hope that he would pick up this time. She walked back to the car and picked up her phone. As she dialled his number her phone made a squeaking noise and the light drained from the screen. Her battery was dead.

No no no! What was she going to do now? She was close to Fergus' house and she remembered the

GPS instructions well enough to walk there, but she was almost three miles away still. To walk would take well over an hour with the snow and her heeled boots.

"Ah," she cried to the air as she dropped her phone on the driver's seat.

Ella leant against her car and tried to construct a plan. She wondered how likely it was that someone would pass by the road. She hadn't seen another car on the road since she left the motorway but hopefully someone would be coming this way, travelling to a Christmas Day church service or to visit their relatives.

Ella stared at the cog that she was still holding. She didn't want to throw it back on to the ground or over the hedge into the field in case it damaged another vehicle or hurt an animal. She walked to the back of her car and opened the boot. She dropped the piece of machinery in and moved aside some canvases and sketches that were strewn untidily across the boot to feel for a latch. Ella felt something that was colder than the carpeted floor of the boot and yanked on it. It was a plastic lever that opened a hidden compartment. Inside it was a spare tyre. *Hurrah!*

Ella was filled with hope as she hoisted out the spare tyre and put it on the snowy floor. She felt for the wrench and jack and stared at them in her hands. She had never changed a tyre before but she had seen her brother change the tyre on his motorbike many times. Suddenly she felt very glad of all the hours she had spent annoying Jimi by hanging around the garage as he worked on his bike. She could do this!

Ella put her car into first gear then walked to the rear left wheel and started to remove the hubcap. She rested her left knee on the cold road while partially loosening the lug nuts with the wrench. She didn't have anything big and heavy she could use as a stopper on one of the wheels to prevent the car from rolling so she hoped for the best. She took off her coat and crouched down in the snow. She inserted the handle in the jack and turned it clockwise to lift the car up. Once it was high enough, she pulled off the lug nuts completely and took off the flat tyre. She chucked it onto the floor behind her and picked up the spare tyre. She was impressed with how she had done so far but now she was faced with a new problem; which way around did the tyre go on?

Ella surveyed the tyre and decided it looked right for the air valve to be on the outside. She slid on the new tyre and put the lug nuts back on, tightening them in the same order she had undone them. She stood back and sighed. She was shattered; the tyre was so heavy and the floor was so cold she felt like collapsing in the snow and crying. What a Christmas it had been so far! She just needed to wind down the jack until the tyre touched the floor and she would be done. When she had wound the jack down, she removed it and slung it, and the flat tyre, into her boot. She had done it!

Ella, feeling rather smug and proud of herself, had a new burst of energy. Perhaps this Christmas wasn't going to be so bad after all? She had saved herself and now she was going to save her relationship. Ella put her coat back on, got in the car and started the engine.

*

Fergus' driveway was longer than Ella had expected it to be. It was lined with gigantic oak trees that looked as if they reached right up to the sky. Snowy fields looked magical and reminded her of the set of the *Nutcracker*. Eventually the trees thinned out and the drive opened up into a clearing where a gorgeous Georgian rectory stood. Warm orange light from inside the windows made the golden stone look like it was glowing. Ella stopped her car a few hundred yards before the house and took in its grandeur. The portico, with its extended pillars and black door, was so stately.

Ella was suddenly hit by the stupidity of her trip. Was she going to knock on the front door and just ask whoever opened it if she could see Fergus? Ella drove her car a little further and stopped it next to a collection of bushes on the right of the house. She stepped out of the car sheepishly and could just make out a face looking down at her from one of the bedroom windows at the top of the house. She heard a rustling through the trees to the right of her and footsteps crunching on the gravel. She turned to see Fergus. He was holding a pile of logs in his arms and was using his chin to keep the top logs from falling. He dropped some of the logs on the floor in suprise. Ella smiled nervously.

"Hello."

"Ella! What are you doing here?" he asked bewildered while setting down the logs on the floor. "You look freezing. Your face is blue!"

"I am freezing! Look Fergus, I know this is mad me coming to see you and on Christmas too, but I felt I owed you an explanation. You rushed off so quickly last night and you weren't answering my calls. I couldn't bear to think that you were upset with me."

Fergus' eyes widened. She had his full attention so she moved one step closer to him.

"The man who showed up last night and at my exhibition is called Robbie Newton. He is my ex-boyfriend." Ella explained her entire history with Robbie in as few words as she could. She told Fergus about their break-up and how Robbie had returned to propose to her. She explained that nothing had happened between them last night; she had put Robbie to bed on her sofa and this morning they had left things amicably. Then she had decided to drive to Fergus' house to explain the whole situation to him, although a flat tyre had held her back.

"I didn't tell you at the exhibition who he was because I didn't want to drag him into our new relationship and I didn't know why he was back. I met with him on Saturday night to understand why he had come back and to finally talk with him face to face about the end of our relationship. I never expected him to propose and I didn't foresee the kiss. Foolishly, I got caught up in the moment, but I knew as soon as I kissed him that it was wrong. I said no to his proposal straight away and I actually ran out of the restaurant laughing because I could see so clearly what I wanted. I was happy in the knowledge that there was only one person I wanted to see and kiss." Ella stepped closer to Fergus now and put her hands on his upper arms and looked into his eyes as she spoke. "I know we haven't known each other long and you must think I'm bonkers for coming here but … well, I'm falling for you. And I would like nothing more than for us to be together."

Relief washed over Fergus as he noticeably relaxed. He smiled and pulled her in close to his chest. Ella could see figures forming in the window behind him but she didn't care. Right now, she just wanted to be held by Fergus. He looked down at her frozen face with such tenderness.

"Oh Ella," he said finally. "I have completely and utterly fallen for you too. I love you," he whispered as he brushed a curl from over her eye.

"I love you too," she said with sheer happiness. Fergus dipped down to kiss Ella and ran his hand through her icy hair. Their eyes locked and they smiled at each other until Fergus spoke again. "I'm sorry I left so suddenly last night and didn't answer your calls. I thought it was best to remove myself from the equation. I thought that perhaps I was holding you back from saying yes and if I stepped back you'd be able to make your decision guilt free. I guess I was trying to be noble about it but it was killing me not knowing what was happening."

"I didn't want to say yes Fergus," she said, nuzzling into the warmth of his neck. "I wanted you."

"I'm so glad you did. And I can't believe you drove all the way out here for me and had to change a tyre in the snow!"

Ella laughed and stepped back from him.

"Now, I'm sure my family are dying to meet the mysterious girl I'm kissing in the drive. Let's go inside."

"That's so sweet of you, but I can't gate-crash your Christmas Fergus. I just came to tell — "

"Nonsense Ell. You're freezing and I want to spend Christmas with you. Let's go in and drink something to warm you up. My mum makes an excellent eggnog..." he said in a coaxing voice.

Ella giggled and kissed him on the cheek.

"What is so funny?" Fergus asked as a smile spread through his silvery stubble.

Eggnog. Eggnog was funny. Little did Fergus know that only minutes before they had bumped into each other in the supermarket, Ella had been thinking about eggnog.

"Nothing," she said sweetly. "I was just thinking that *this Christmas* is already the best Christmas I've ever had."

Printed in Great Britain
by Amazon.co.uk, Ltd.,
Marston Gate.